THE SECRET LIFE OF PETS

STÉPHANE LAPUSS' **GOUM**

WRITTEN BY:
STÉPHANE LAPUSS'

ART BY:
GOUM

ENGLISH TRANSLATION:
MONTANA KANE

TITAN COMICS

Senior Creative Editor
DAVID LEACH

Managing Editor
MARTIN EDEN

Designer
DAN BURA

Production Controller
PETER JAMES

Senior Production Controller
JACKIE FLOOK

Art Director
OZ BROWNE

Sales & Circulation Manager
STEVE TOTHILL

SeniorPublicist
WILLIAM O'MULLANE

Publicist
IMOGEN HARRIS

Ad & Marketing Assistant
BELLA HOY

Commercial Manager
MICHELLE FAIRLAMB

Publishing Director
DARRYL TOTHILL

Operations Director
LEIGH BAULCH

Executive Director
VIVIAN CHEUNG

Publisher
NICK LANDAU

SECRET LIFE OF PETS
JUNE 2019. Published by Titan Comics, a division of Titan Publishing Group, Ltd. 144 Southwark Street, London SE1 0UP. Titan Comics is a registered tradedmark of Titan Publishing Group, Ltd. All rights reserved.© 2019 - The Secret Life of Pets and all related marks and characters are trademarks and copyrights of Universal Studios. Licensed by Universal Studios. All rights reserved. Licensed by Universal Studios Licensing LLC, 2019. All Rights Reserved. TCN 3549 A CIP catalogue record for this title is available from the British Library.

PRINTED IN CANADA
10 9 8 7 6 5 4 3 2 1

ISBN: 9781787732179

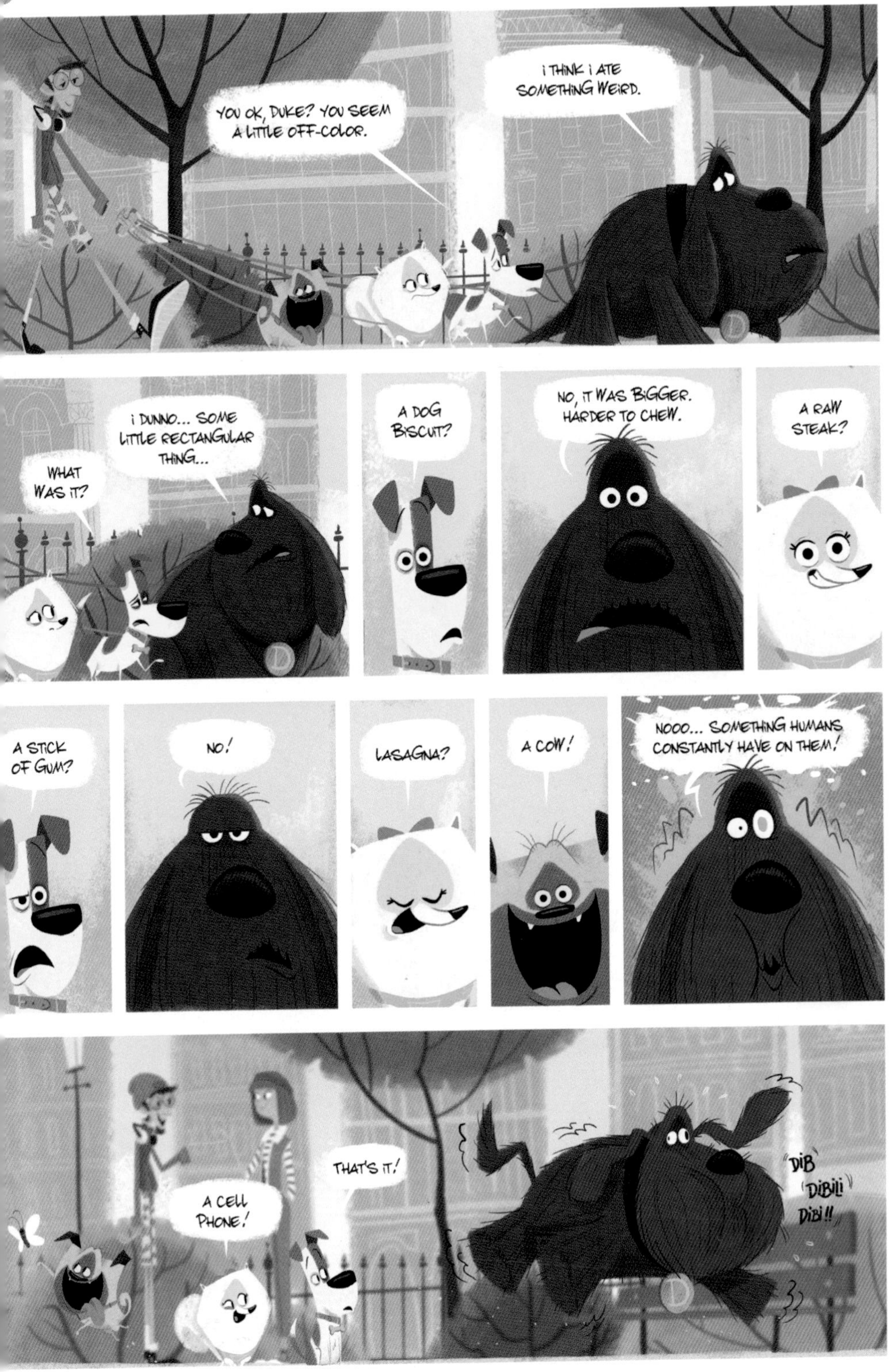
YOU OK, DUKE? YOU SEEM A LITTLE OFF-COLOR.
I THINK I ATE SOMETHING WEIRD.
WHAT WAS IT?
I DUNNO... SOME LITTLE RECTANGULAR THING...
A DOG BISCUIT?
NO, IT WAS BIGGER. HARDER TO CHEW.
A RAW STEAK?
A STICK OF GUM?
NO!
LASAGNA?
A COW!
NOOO... SOMETHING HUMANS CONSTANTLY HAVE ON THEM!
A CELL PHONE!
THAT'S IT!
DIB DIBILI DIBI!!

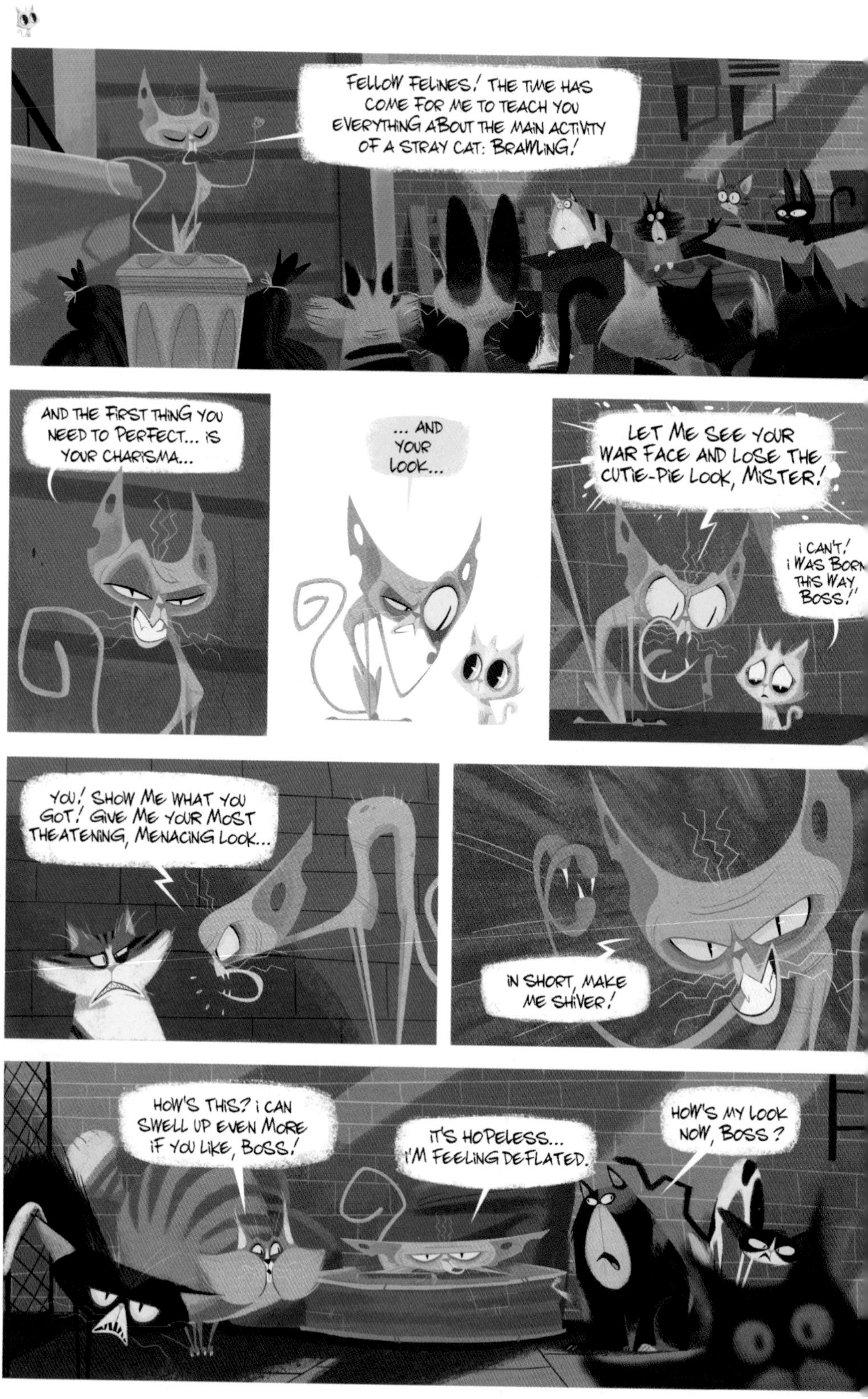
FELLOW FELINES! THE TIME HAS COME FOR ME TO TEACH YOU EVERYTHING ABOUT THE MAIN ACTIVITY OF A STRAY CAT: BRAWLING!
AND THE FIRST THING YOU NEED TO PERFECT... IS YOUR CHARISMA...
... AND YOUR LOOK...
LET ME SEE YOUR WAR FACE AND LOSE THE CUTIE-PIE LOOK, MISTER!
I CAN'T! I WAS BORN THIS WAY, BOSS!
YOU! SHOW ME WHAT YOU GOT! GIVE ME YOUR MOST THEATENING, MENACING LOOK...
IN SHORT, MAKE ME SHIVER!
HOW'S THIS? I CAN SWELL UP EVEN MORE IF YOU LIKE, BOSS!
IT'S HOPELESS... I'M FEELING DEFLATED.
HOW'S MY LOOK NOW, BOSS?

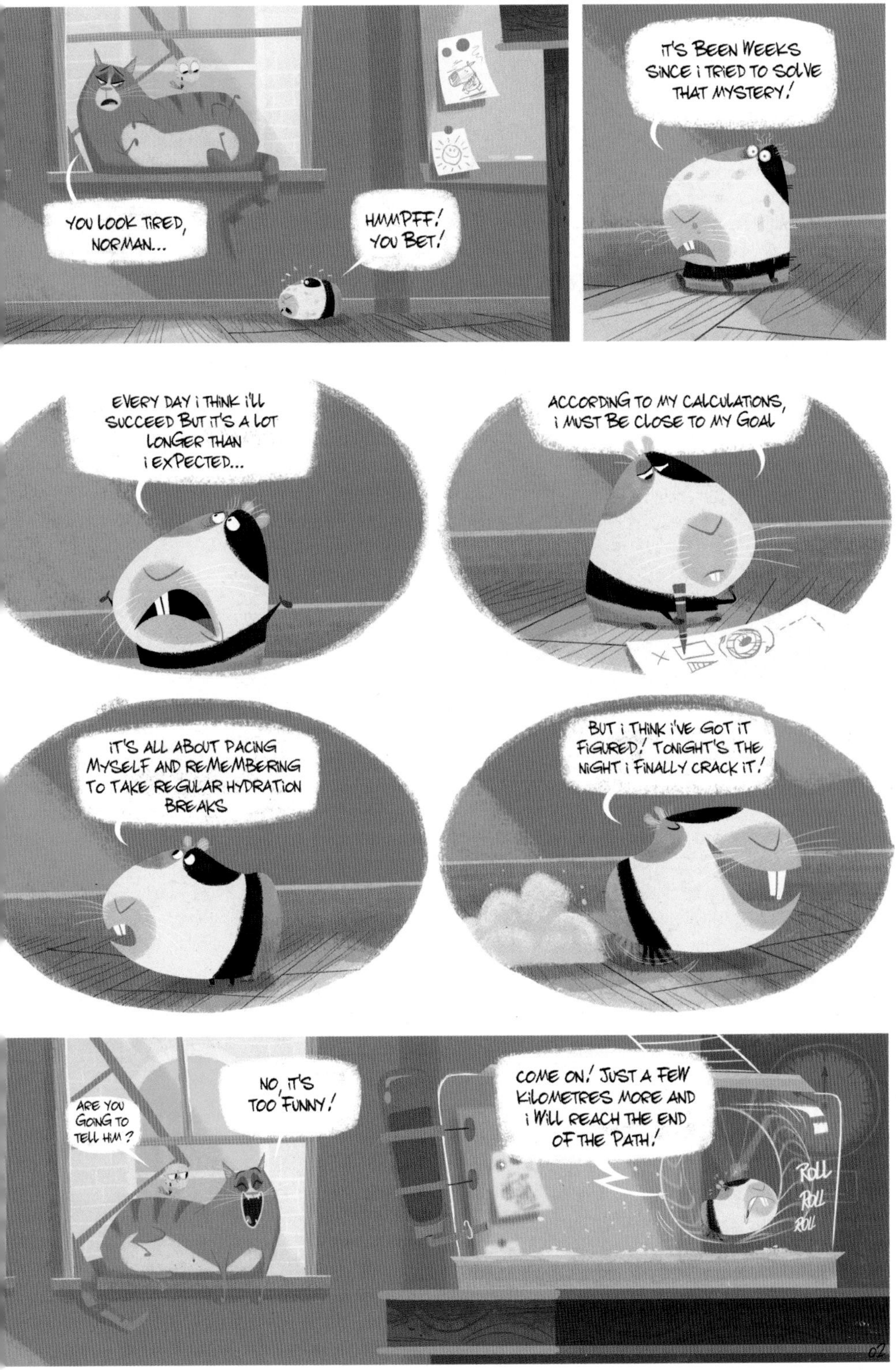
YOU LOOK TIRED, NORMAN...
HMMPFF! YOU BET!
IT'S BEEN WEEKS SINCE I TRIED TO SOLVE THAT MYSTERY!
EVERY DAY I THINK I'LL SUCCEED BUT IT'S A LOT LONGER THAN I EXPECTED...
ACCORDING TO MY CALCULATIONS, I MUST BE CLOSE TO MY GOAL
IT'S ALL ABOUT PACING MYSELF AND REMEMBERING TO TAKE REGULAR HYDRATION BREAKS
BUT I THINK I'VE GOT IT FIGURED! TONIGHT'S THE NIGHT I FINALLY CRACK IT!
ARE YOU GOING TO TELL HIM?
NO, IT'S TOO FUNNY!
COME ON! JUST A FEW KILOMETRES MORE AND I WILL REACH THE END OF THE PATH!
ROLL
ROLL
ROLL

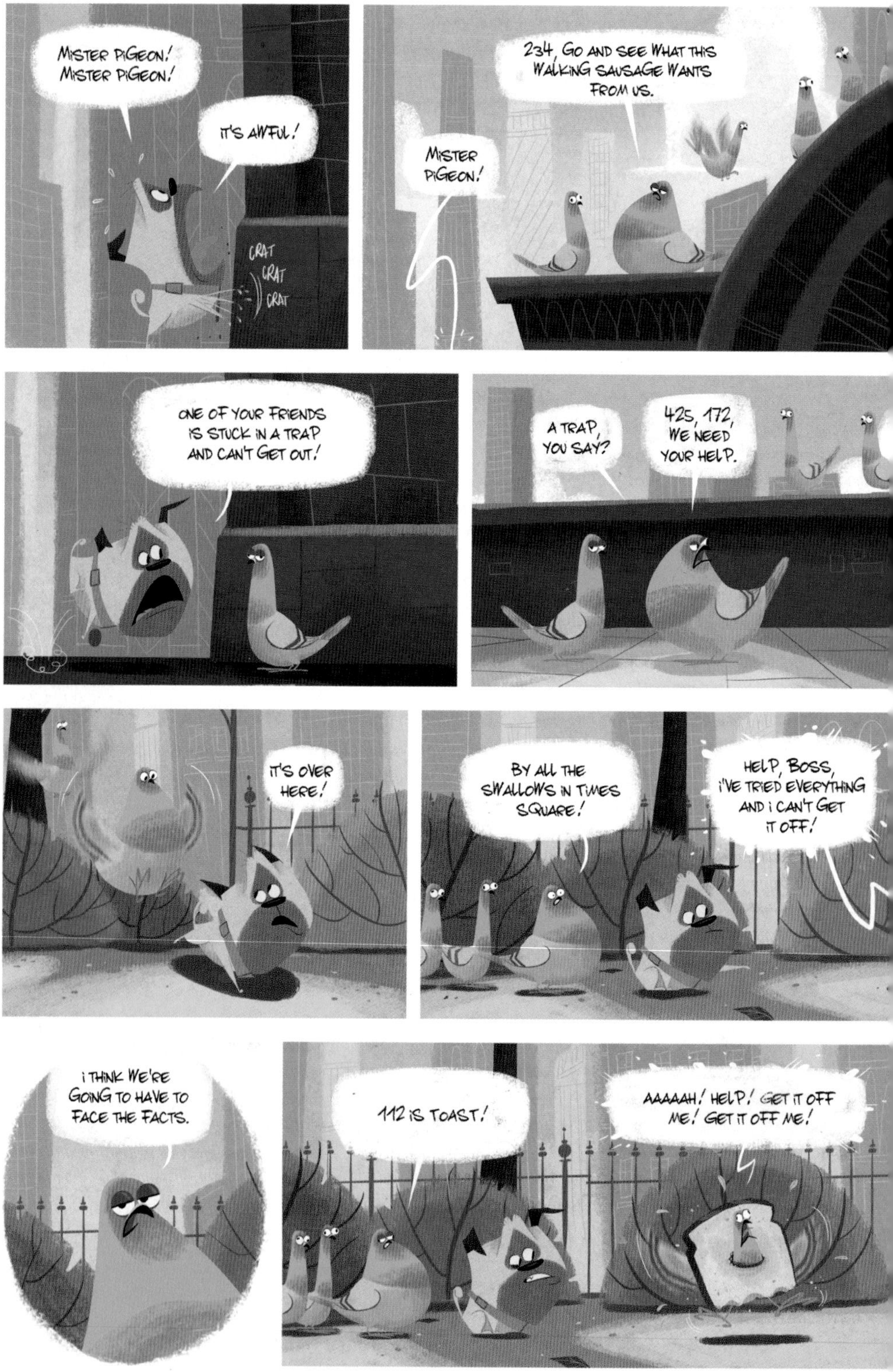
MISTER PIGEON! MISTER PIGEON!
IT'S AWFUL!
CRAT
CRAT
CRAT
MISTER PIGEON!
234, GO AND SEE WHAT THIS WALKING SAUSAGE WANTS FROM US.
ONE OF YOUR FRIENDS IS STUCK IN A TRAP AND CAN'T GET OUT!
A TRAP, YOU SAY?
425, 172, WE NEED YOUR HELP.
IT'S OVER HERE!
BY ALL THE SWALLOWS IN TIMES SQUARE!
HELP, BOSS, I'VE TRIED EVERYTHING AND I CAN'T GET IT OFF!
I THINK WE'RE GOING TO HAVE TO FACE THE FACTS.
112 IS TOAST!
AAAAAH! HELP! GET IT OFF ME! GET IT OFF ME!

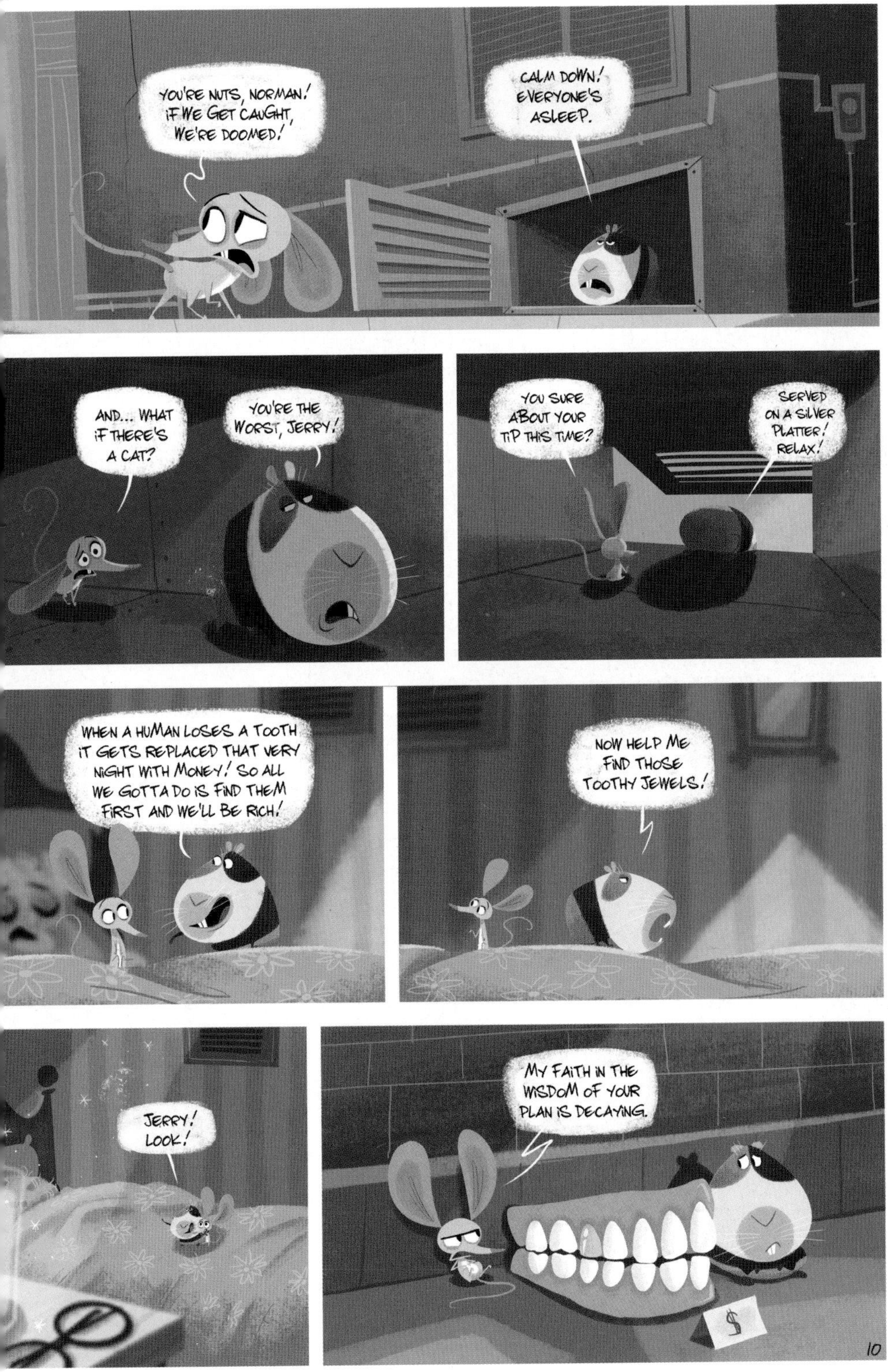
YOU'RE NUTS, NORMAN! IF WE GET CAUGHT, WE'RE DOOMED!
CALM DOWN! EVERYONE'S ASLEEP.
AND... WHAT IF THERE'S A CAT?
YOU'RE THE WORST, JERRY!
YOU SURE ABOUT YOUR TIP THIS TIME?
SERVED ON A SILVER PLATTER! RELAX!
WHEN A HUMAN LOSES A TOOTH IT GETS REPLACED THAT VERY NIGHT WITH MONEY! SO ALL WE GOTTA DO IS FIND THEM FIRST AND WE'LL BE RICH!
NOW HELP ME FIND THOSE TOOTHY JEWELS!
JERRY! LOOK!
MY FAITH IN THE WISDOM OF YOUR PLAN IS DECAYING.
$
10

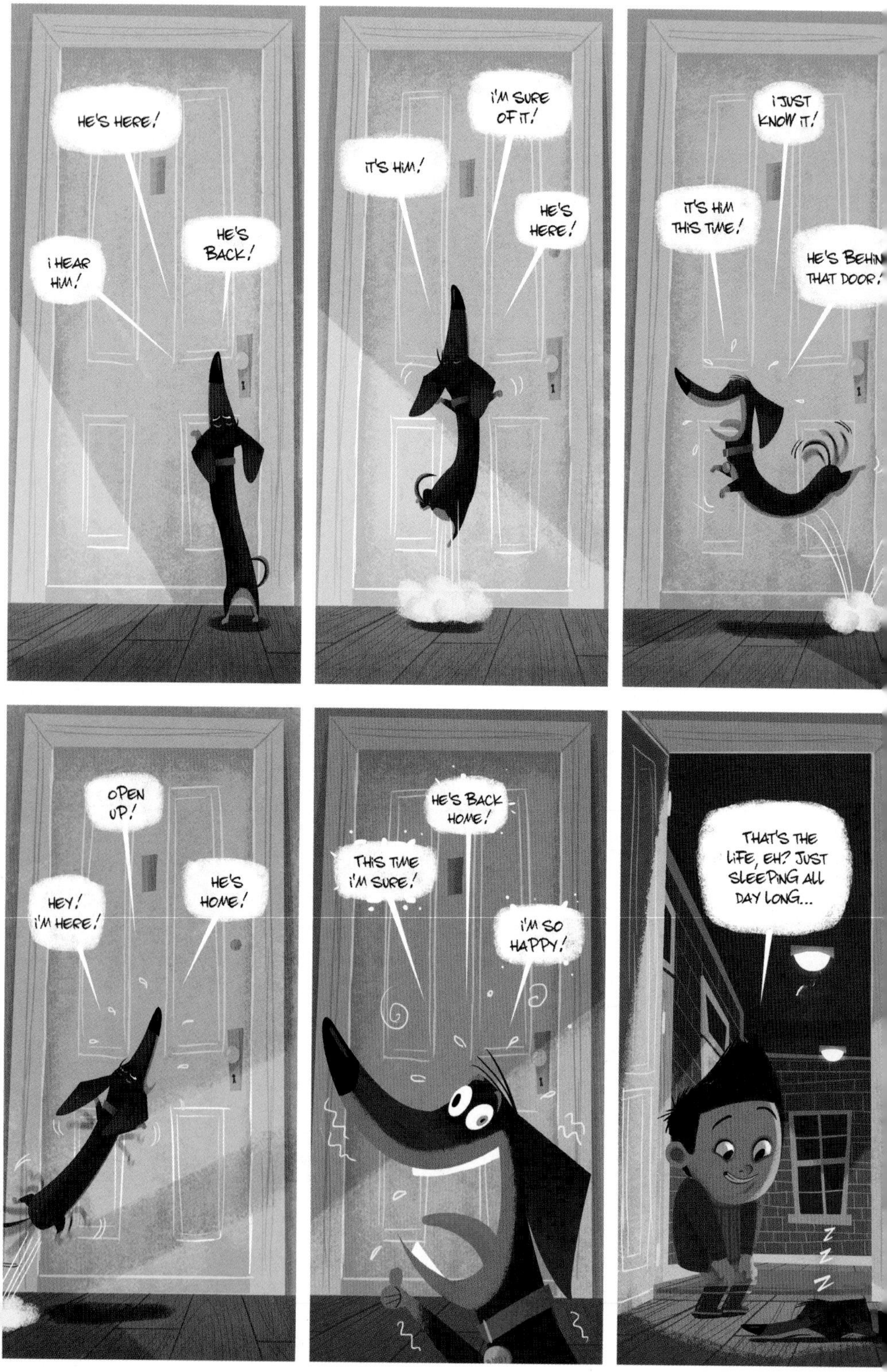
HE'S HERE!
i HEAR HiM!
HE'S BACK!
iT'S HiM!
i'M SURE OF iT!
HE'S HERE!
i JUST KNOW iT!
iT'S HiM THiS TiME!
HE'S BEHIN
THAT DOOR!
OPEN UP!
HEY! i'M HERE!
HE'S HOME!
THiS TiME i'M SURE!
HE'S BACK HOME!
i'M SO HAPPY!
THAT'S THE LiFE, EH? JUST SLEEPiNG ALL DAY LONG...
Z
Z
Z

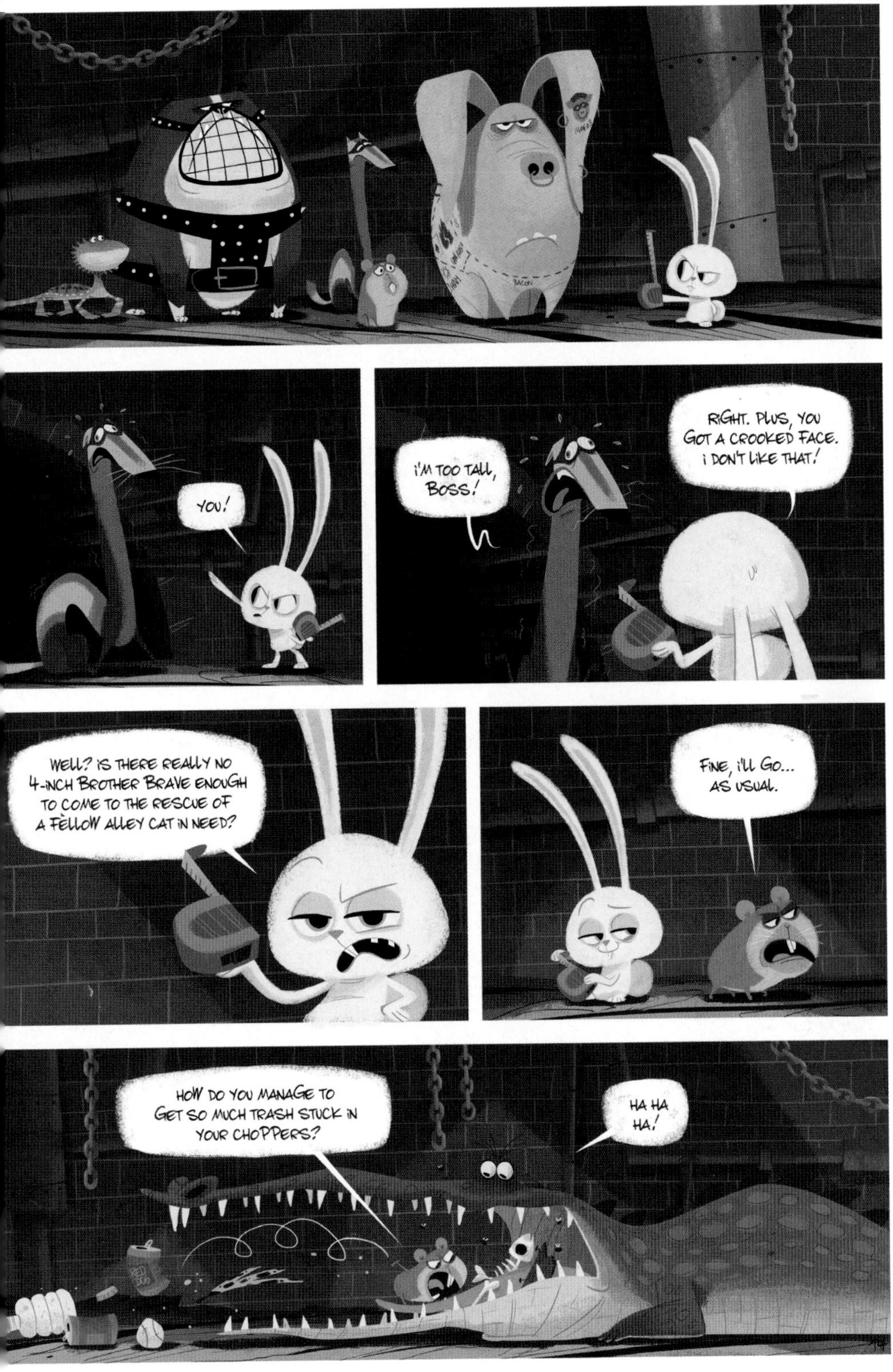
YOU!
I'M TOO TALL, BOSS!
RIGHT. PLUS, YOU GOT A CROOKED FACE. I DON'T LIKE THAT!
WELL? IS THERE REALLY NO 4-INCH BROTHER BRAVE ENOUGH TO COME TO THE RESCUE OF A FELLOW ALLEY CAT IN NEED?
FINE, I'LL GO... AS USUAL.
HOW DO YOU MANAGE TO GET SO MUCH TRASH STUCK IN YOUR CHOPPERS?
HA HA HA!

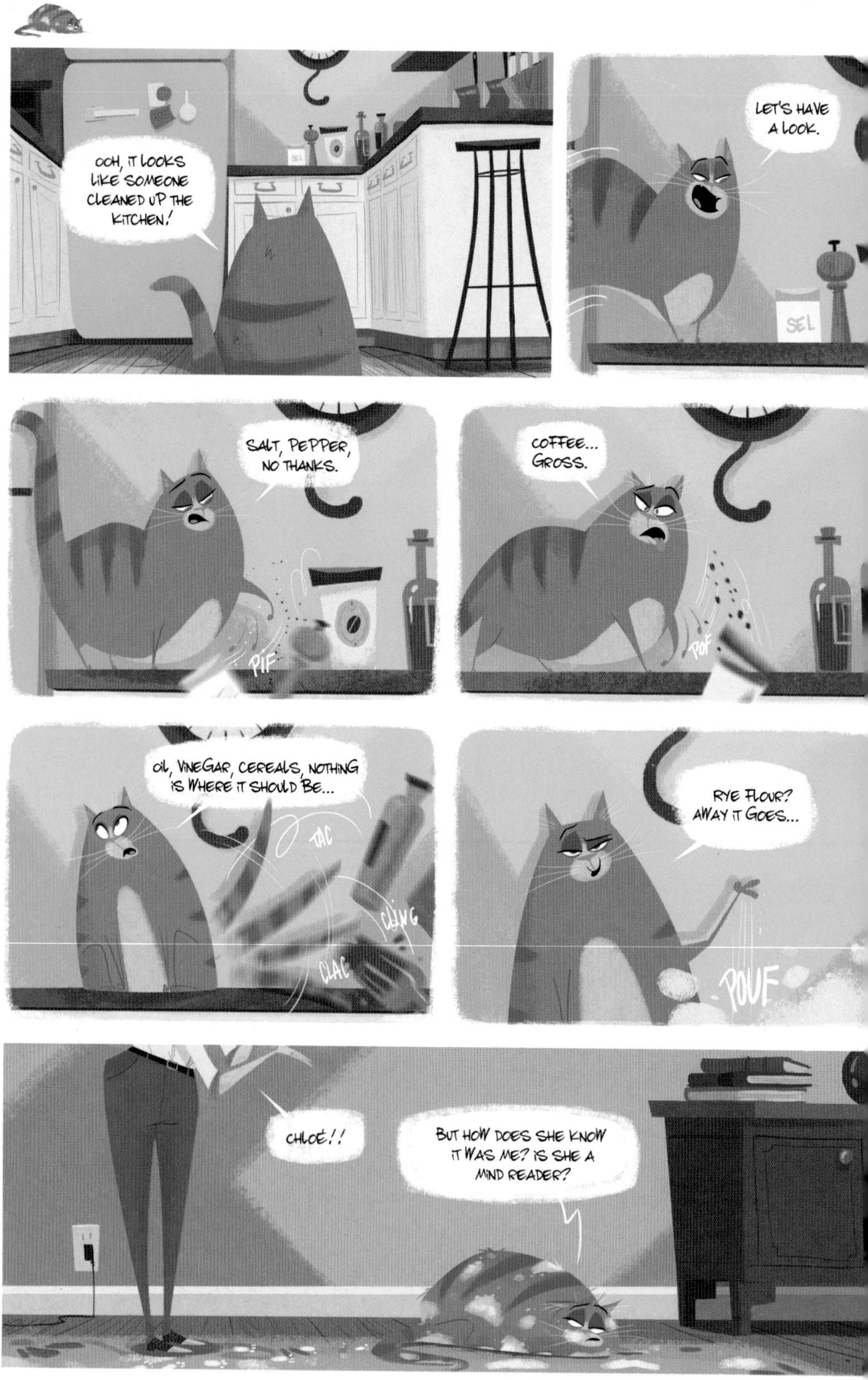
OOH, IT LOOKS LIKE SOMEONE CLEANED UP THE KITCHEN!
LET'S HAVE A LOOK.
SEL
SALT, PEPPER, NO THANKS.
PIF
COFFEE... GROSS.
POF
OIL, VINEGAR, CEREALS, NOTHING IS WHERE IT SHOULD BE...
TAC
CLING
CLAC
RYE FLOUR? AWAY IT GOES...
POUF
CHLOÉ!!
BUT HOW DOES SHE KNOW IT WAS ME? IS SHE A MIND READER?

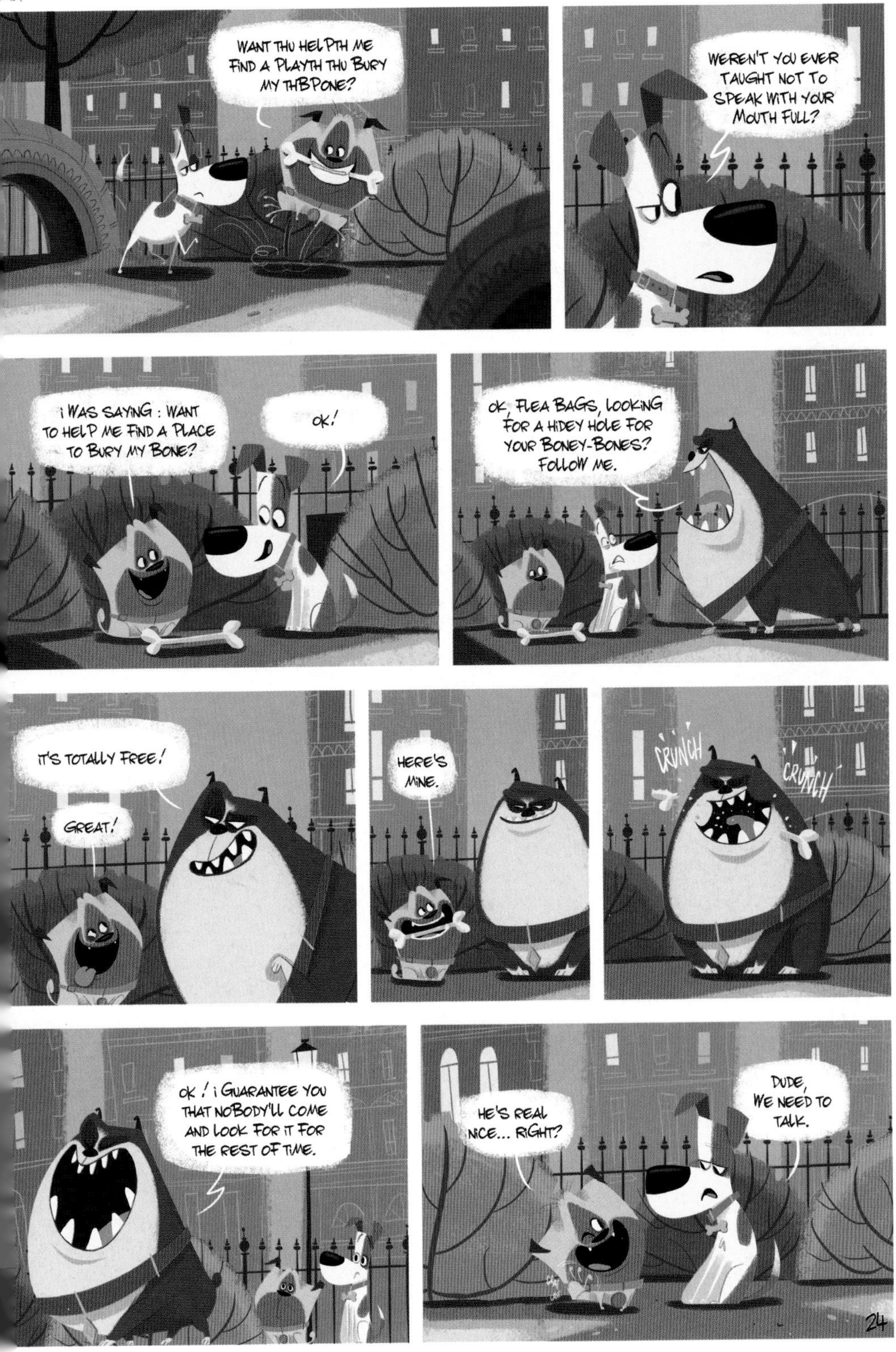
WANT THU HELPTH ME FIND A PLAYTH THU BURY MY THBPONE?
WEREN'T YOU EVER TAUGHT NOT TO SPEAK WITH YOUR MOUTH FULL?
I WAS SAYING : WANT TO HELP ME FIND A PLACE TO BURY MY BONE?
OK!
OK, FLEA BAGS, LOOKING FOR A HIDEY HOLE FOR YOUR BONEY-BONES? FOLLOW ME.
IT'S TOTALLY FREE!
GREAT!
HERE'S MINE.
CRUNCH
CRUNCH
OK! I GUARANTEE YOU THAT NOBODY'LL COME AND LOOK FOR IT FOR THE REST OF TIME.
HE'S REAL NICE... RIGHT?
DUDE, WE NEED TO TALK.
24

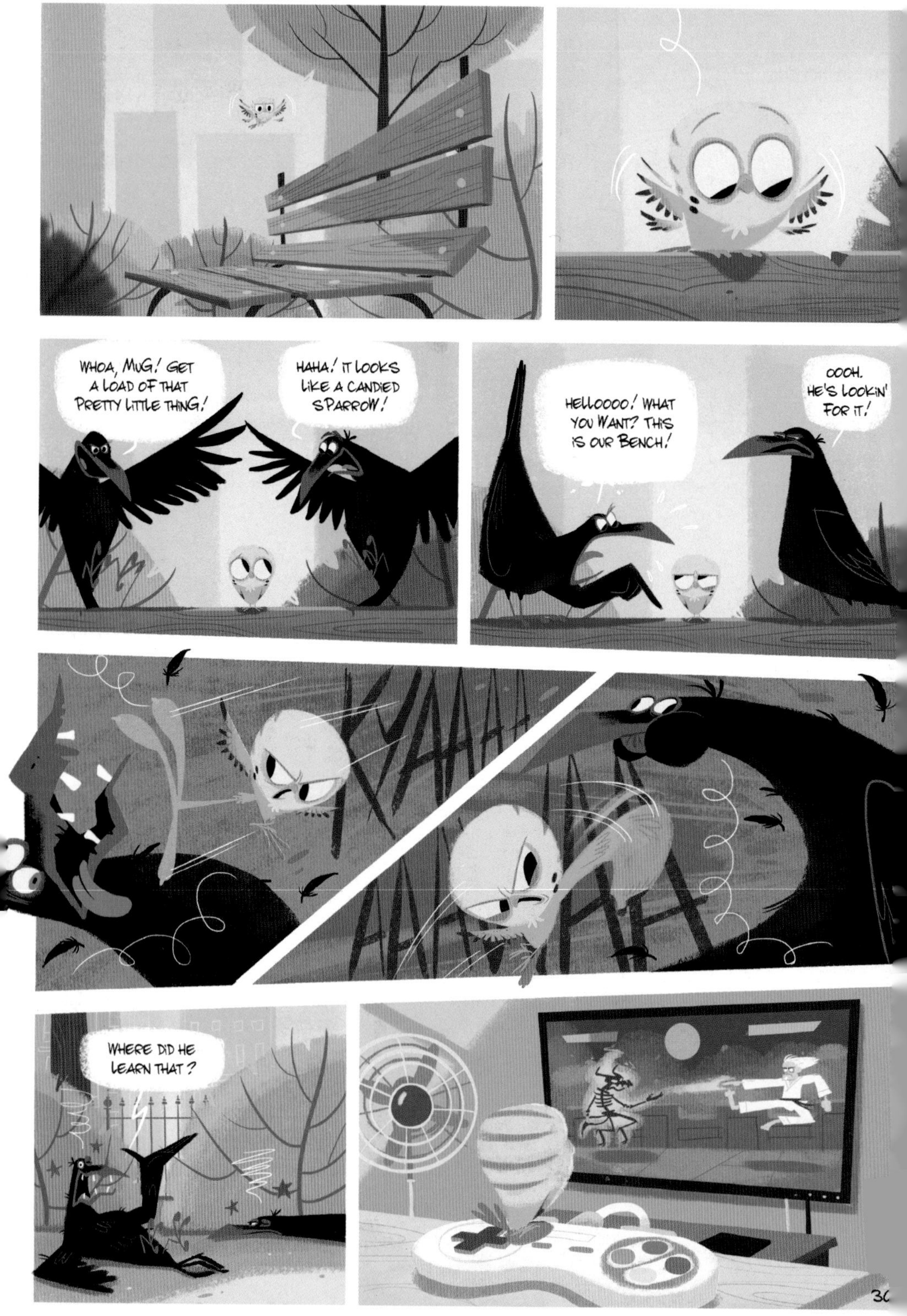
WHOA, MUG! GET A LOAD OF THAT PRETTY LITTLE THING!
HAHA! IT LOOKS LIKE A CANDIED SPARROW!
HELLOOOO! WHAT YOU WANT? THIS IS OUR BENCH!
OOOH. HE'S LOOKIN' FOR IT!
WHERE DID HE LEARN THAT?

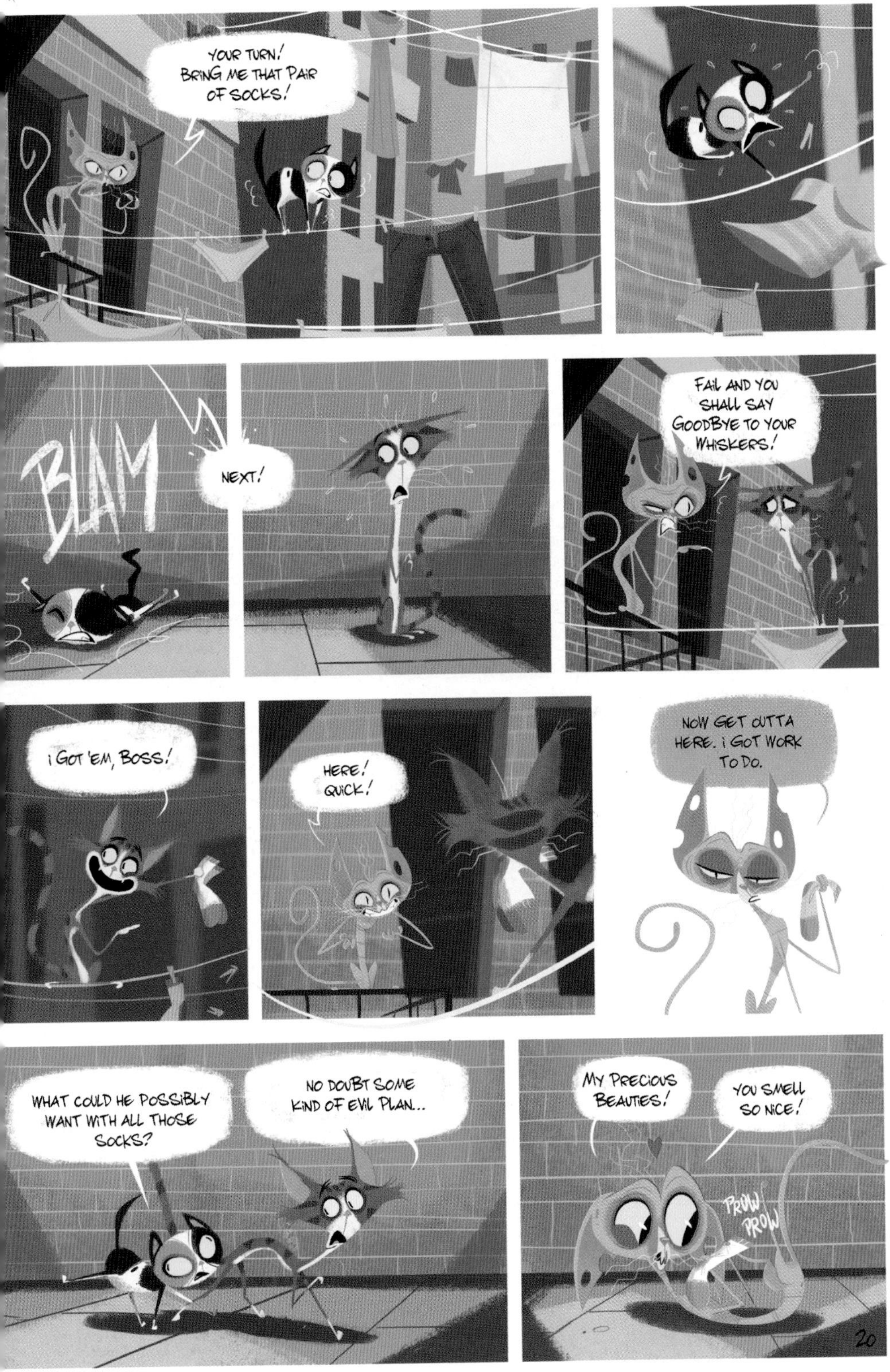
YOUR TURN! BRING ME THAT PAIR OF SOCKS!
BLAM
NEXT!
FAIL AND YOU SHALL SAY GOODBYE TO YOUR WHISKERS!
I GOT 'EM, BOSS!
HERE! QUICK!
NOW GET OUTTA HERE. I GOT WORK TO DO.
WHAT COULD HE POSSIBLY WANT WITH ALL THOSE SOCKS?
NO DOUBT SOME KIND OF EVIL PLAN...
MY PRECIOUS BEAUTIES!
YOU SMELL SO NICE!
PROW PROW
20

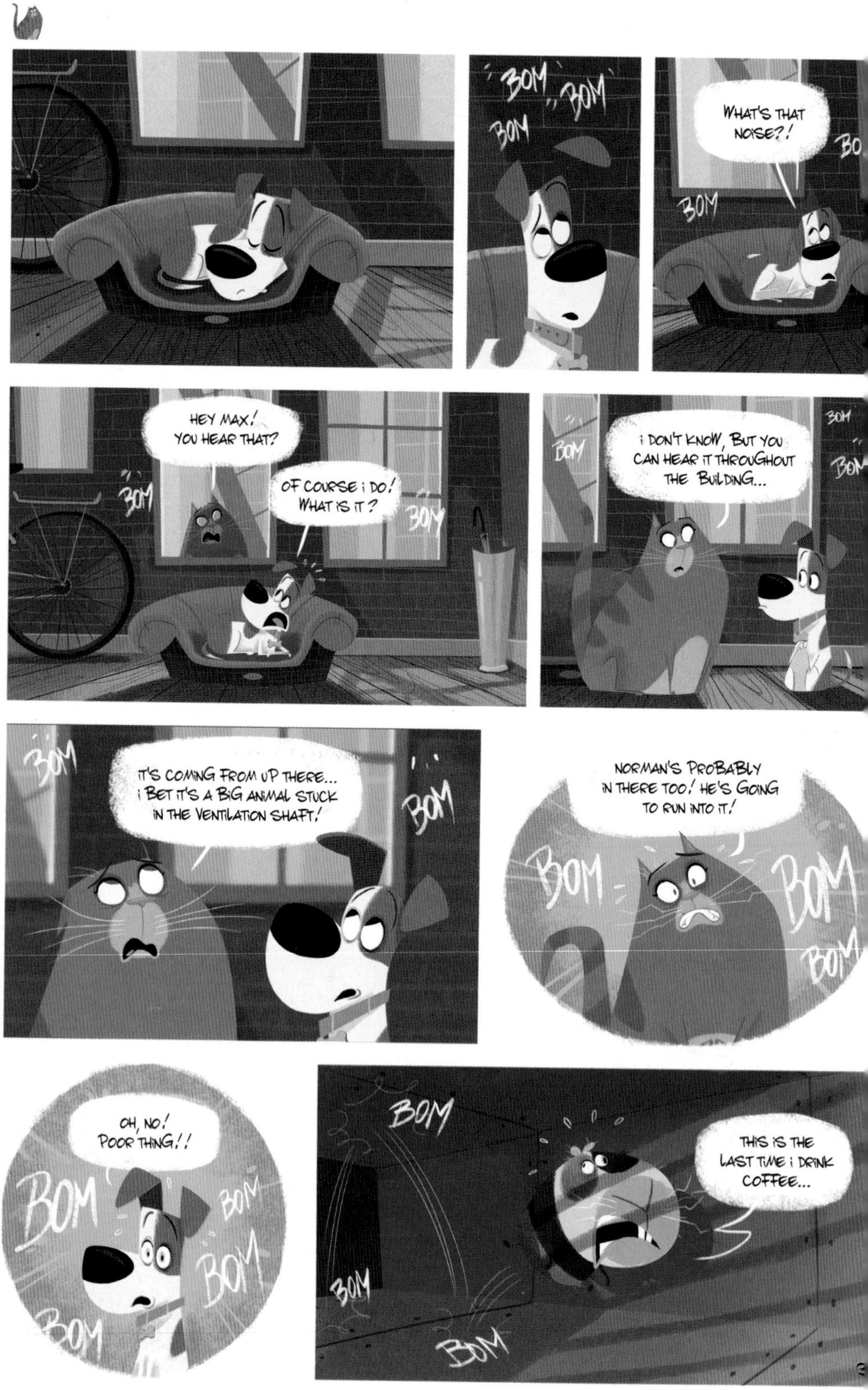

BOM
BOM
BOM
WHAT'S THAT NOISE?!
BOM
BOM
HEY MAX! YOU HEAR THAT?
OF COURSE I DO! WHAT IS IT?
BOM
BOM
BOM
I DON'T KNOW, BUT YOU CAN HEAR IT THROUGHOUT THE BUILDING...
BOM
BOM
BOM
IT'S COMING FROM UP THERE... I BET IT'S A BIG ANIMAL STUCK IN THE VENTILATION SHAFT!
BOM
NORMAN'S PROBABLY IN THERE TOO! HE'S GOING TO RUN INTO IT!
BOM
BOM
BOM
OH, NO! POOR THING!!
BOM
BOM
BOM
BOM
BOM
THIS IS THE LAST TIME I DRINK COFFEE...
BOM
BOM

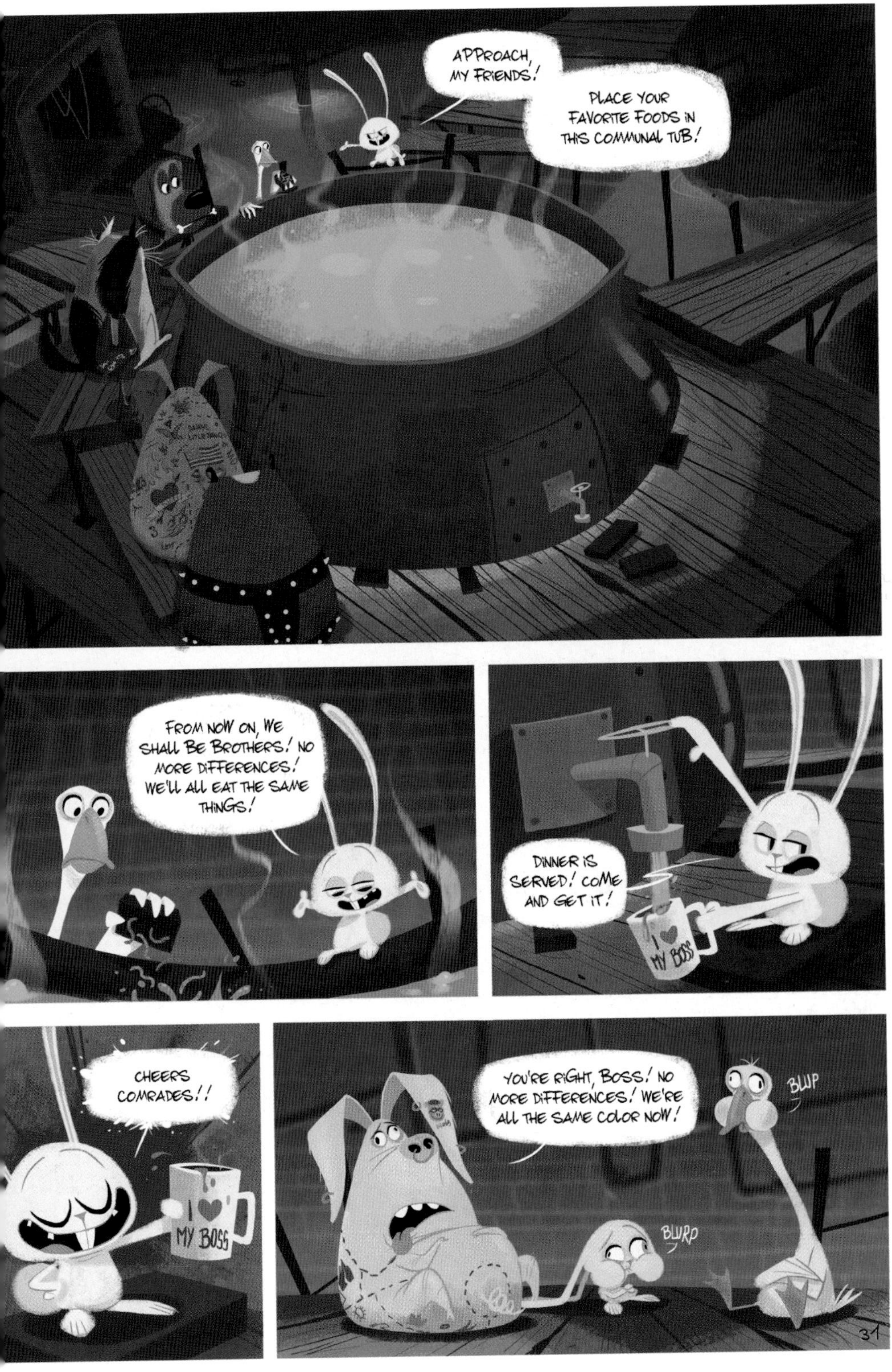
APPROACH, MY FRIENDS!
PLACE YOUR FAVORITE FOODS IN THIS COMMUNAL TUB!
FROM NOW ON, WE SHALL BE BROTHERS! NO MORE DIFFERENCES! WE'LL ALL EAT THE SAME THINGS!
DINNER IS SERVED! COME AND GET IT!
I ♥ MY BOSS
CHEERS COMRADES!!
I ♥ MY BOSS
YOU'RE RIGHT, BOSS! NO MORE DIFFERENCES! WE'RE ALL THE SAME COLOR NOW!
BLUP
BLURP

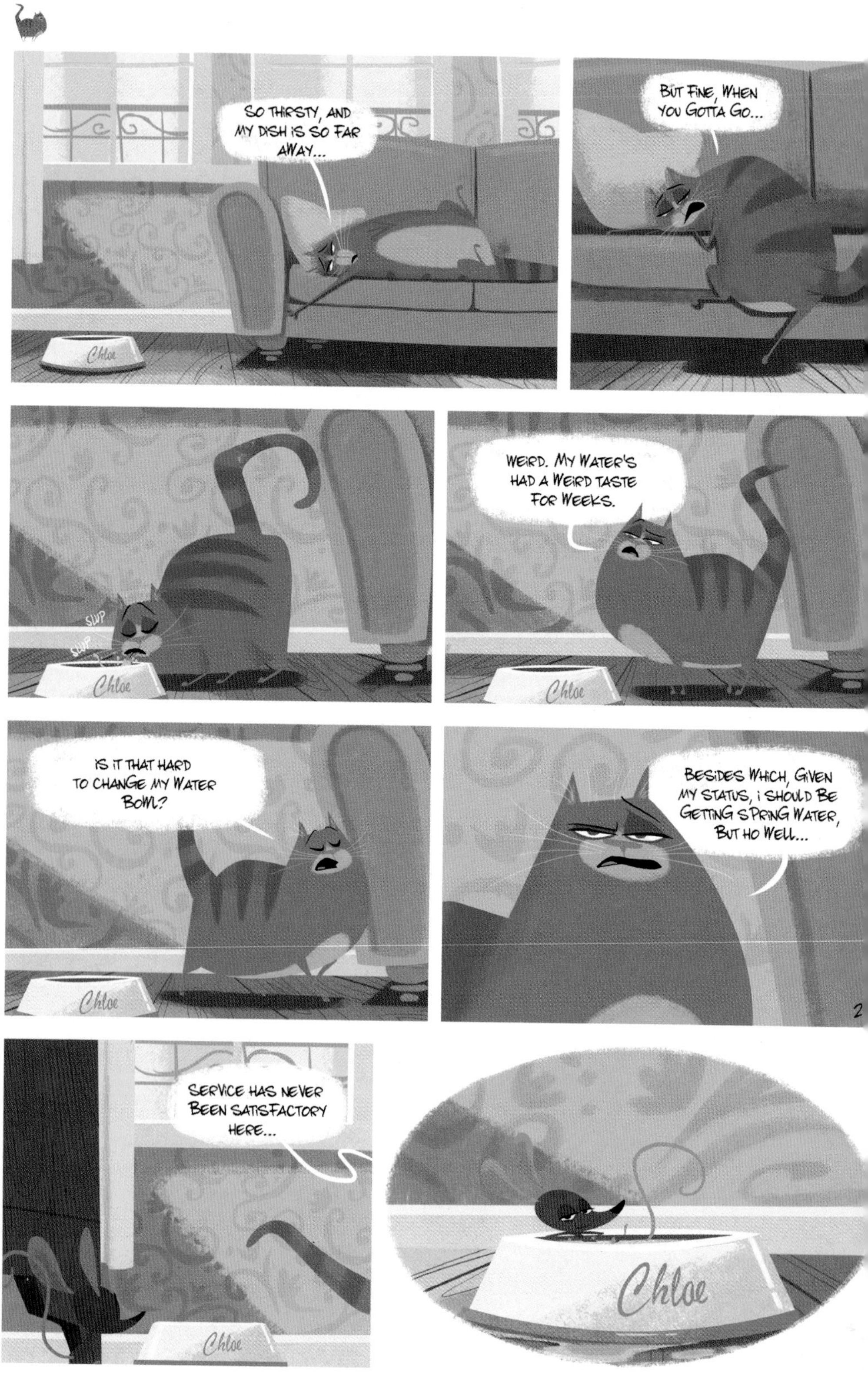
SO THIRSTY, AND MY DISH IS SO FAR AWAY...
Chloe
BUT FINE, WHEN YOU GOTTA GO...
SLUP SLUP
Chloe
WEIRD. MY WATER'S HAD A WEIRD TASTE FOR WEEKS.
Chloe
IS IT THAT HARD TO CHANGE MY WATER BOWL?
Chloe
BESIDES WHICH, GIVEN MY STATUS, I SHOULD BE GETTING SPRING WATER, BUT HO WELL...
SERVICE HAS NEVER BEEN SATISFACTORY HERE...
Chloe
Chloe

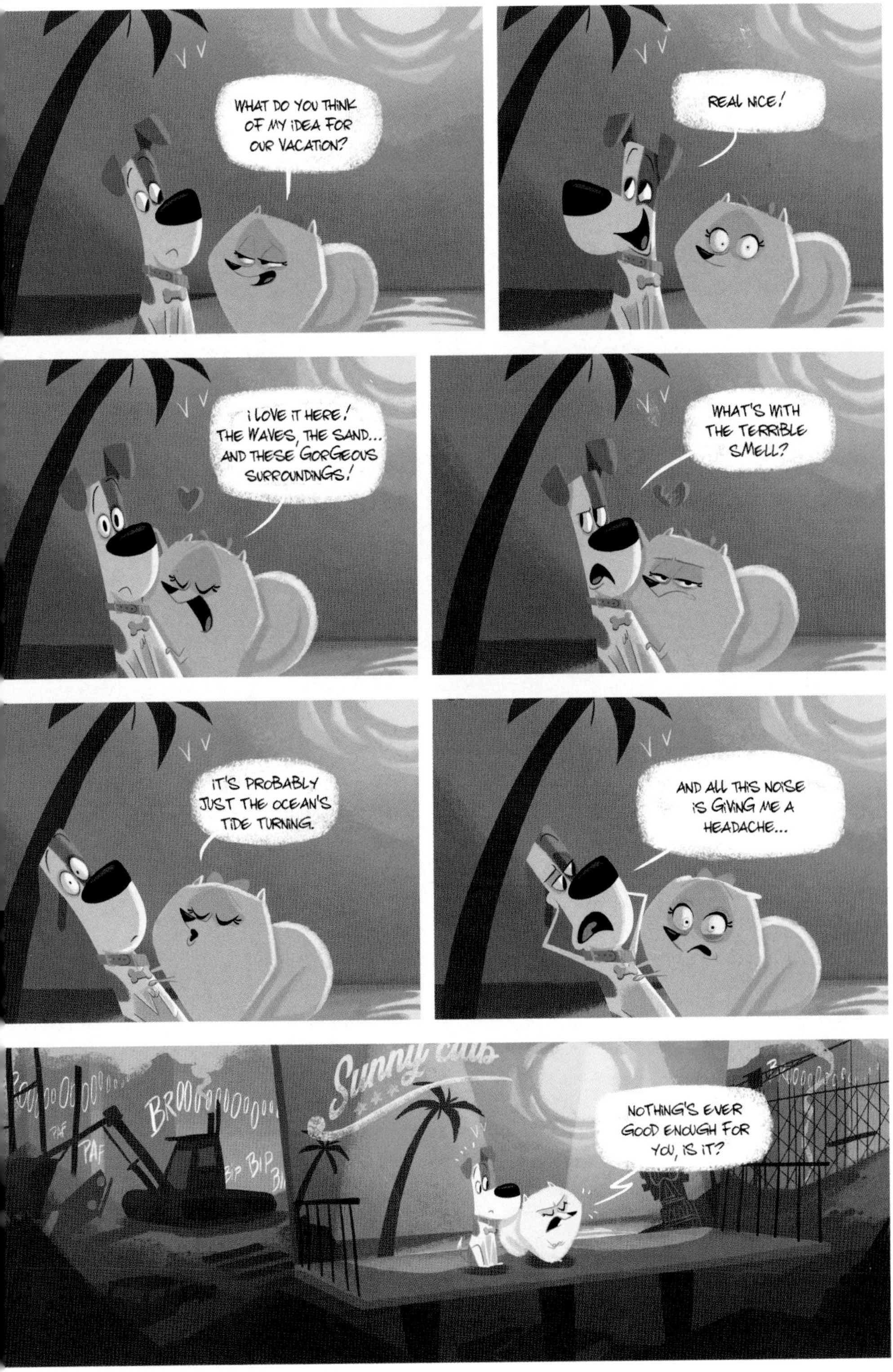
WHAT DO YOU THINK OF MY IDEA FOR OUR VACATION?
REAL NICE!
I LOVE IT HERE! THE WAVES, THE SAND... AND THESE GORGEOUS SURROUNDINGS!
WHAT'S WITH THE TERRIBLE SMELL?
IT'S PROBABLY JUST THE OCEAN'S TIDE TURNING.
AND ALL THIS NOISE IS GIVING ME A HEADACHE...
PAF
BIP BIP
NOTHING'S EVER GOOD ENOUGH FOR YOU, IS IT?

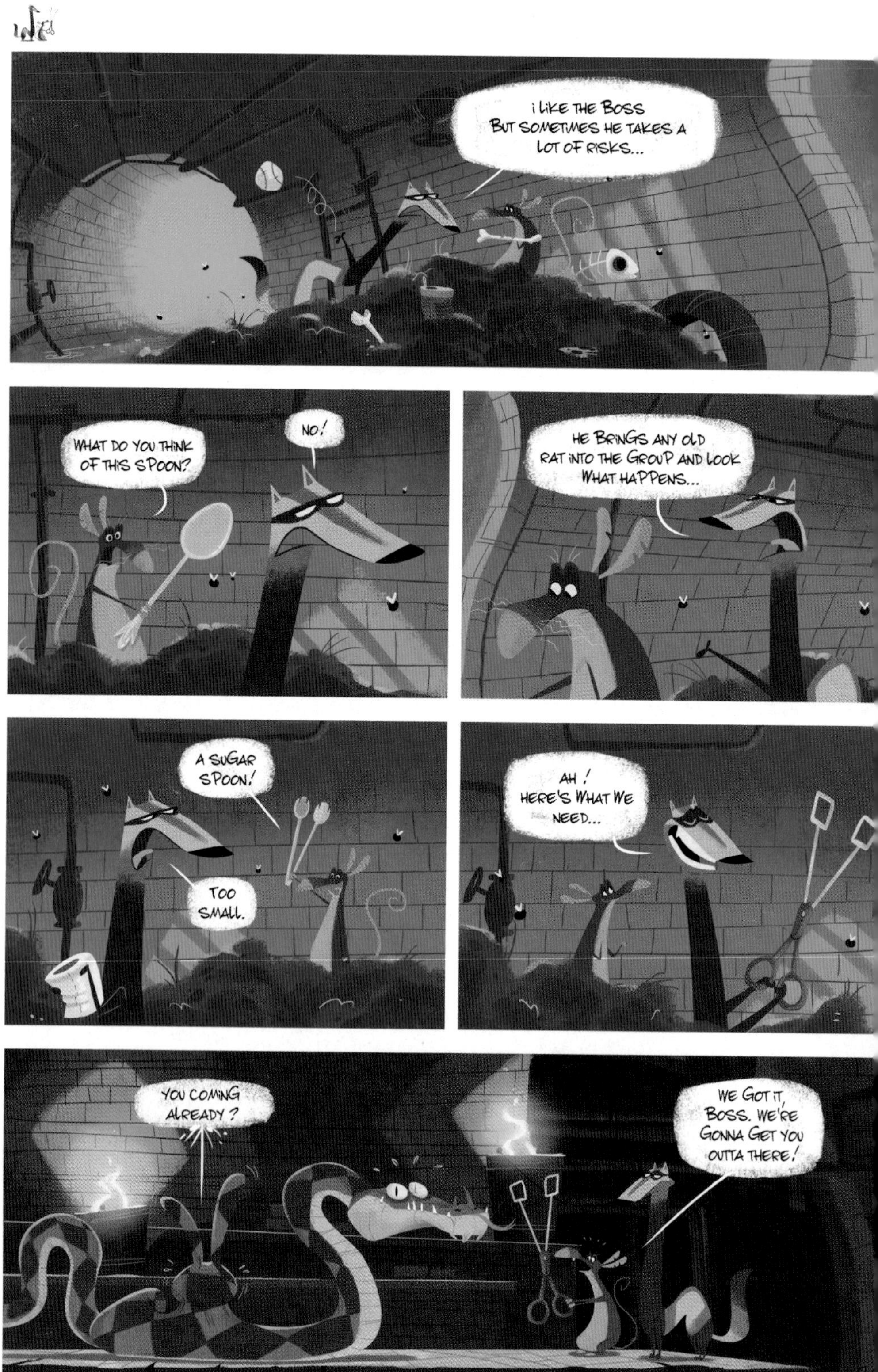
I LIKE THE BOSS BUT SOMETIMES HE TAKES A LOT OF RISKS...
WHAT DO YOU THINK OF THIS SPOON?
NO!
HE BRINGS ANY OLD RAT INTO THE GROUP AND LOOK WHAT HAPPENS...
A SUGAR SPOON!
TOO SMALL.
AH! HERE'S WHAT WE NEED...
YOU COMING ALREADY?
WE GOT IT, BOSS. WE'RE GONNA GET YOU OUTTA THERE!

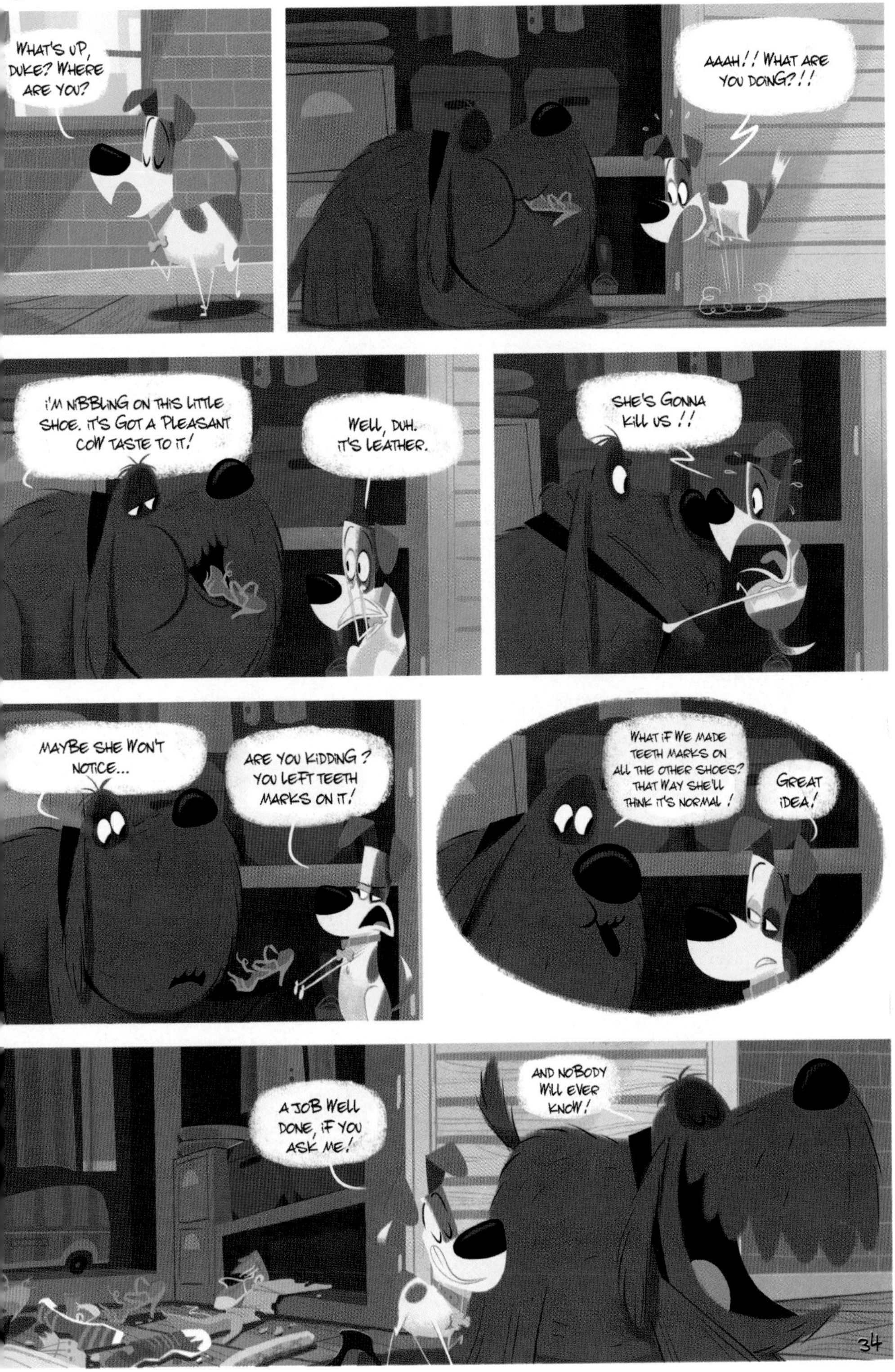
WHAT'S UP, DUKE? WHERE ARE YOU?
AAAH!! WHAT ARE YOU DOING?!!
I'M NIBBLING ON THIS LITTLE SHOE. IT'S GOT A PLEASANT COW TASTE TO IT!
WELL, DUH. IT'S LEATHER.
SHE'S GONNA KILL US!!
MAYBE SHE WON'T NOTICE...
ARE YOU KIDDING? YOU LEFT TEETH MARKS ON IT!
WHAT IF WE MADE TEETH MARKS ON ALL THE OTHER SHOES? THAT WAY SHE'LL THINK IT'S NORMAL!
GREAT IDEA!
A JOB WELL DONE, IF YOU ASK ME!
AND NOBODY WILL EVER KNOW!
34

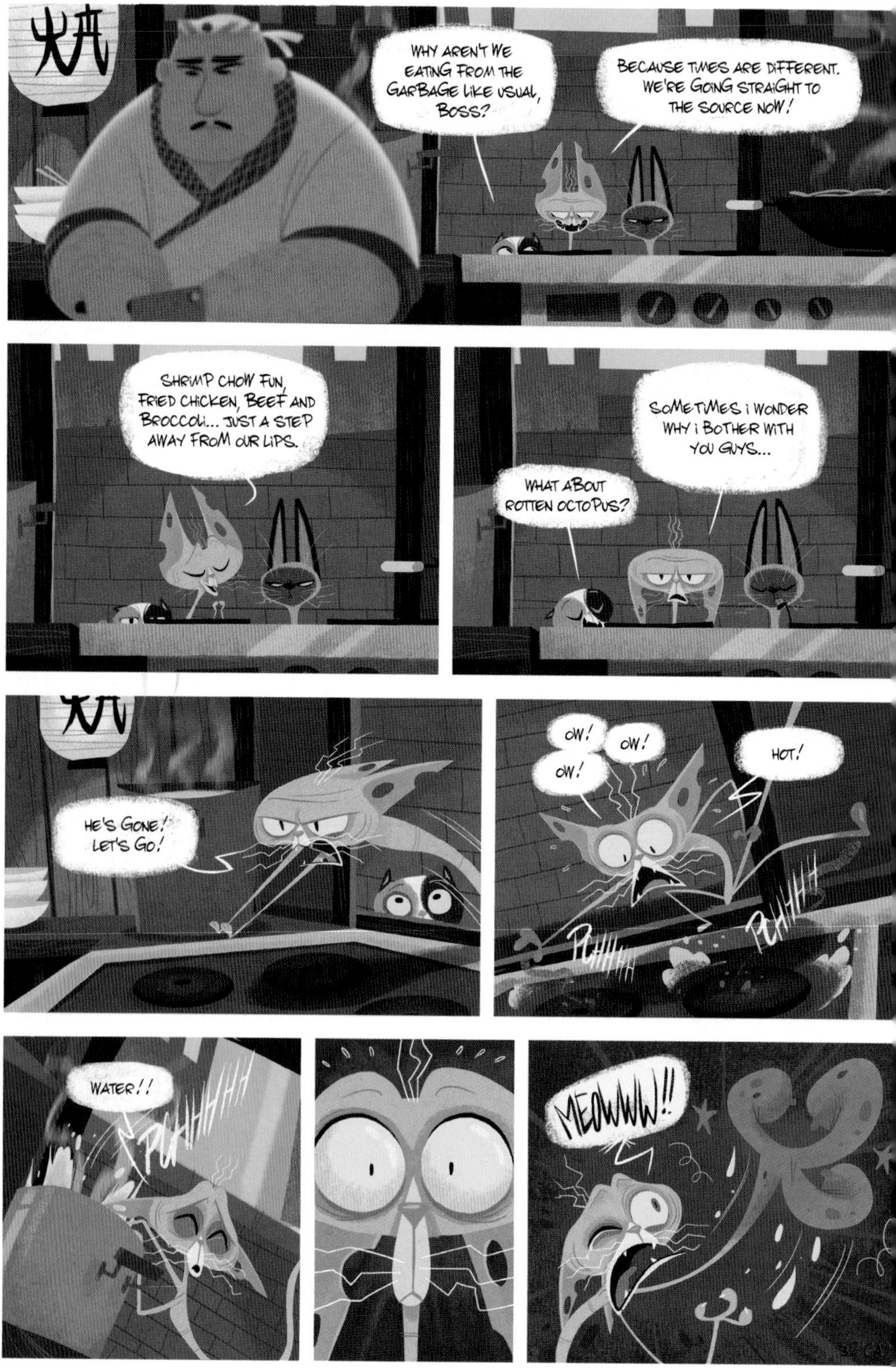

WHY AREN'T WE EATING FROM THE GARBAGE LIKE USUAL, BOSS?
BECAUSE TIMES ARE DIFFERENT. WE'RE GOING STRAIGHT TO THE SOURCE NOW!
SHRIMP CHOW FUN, FRIED CHICKEN, BEEF AND BROCCOLI... JUST A STEP AWAY FROM OUR LIPS.
WHAT ABOUT ROTTEN OCTOPUS?
SOMETIMES I WONDER WHY I BOTHER WITH YOU GUYS...
HE'S GONE! LET'S GO!
OW!
OW!
OW!
HOT!
PCHHHH
PCHHHH
WATER!!
PCHHHHHH
MEOWWW!!

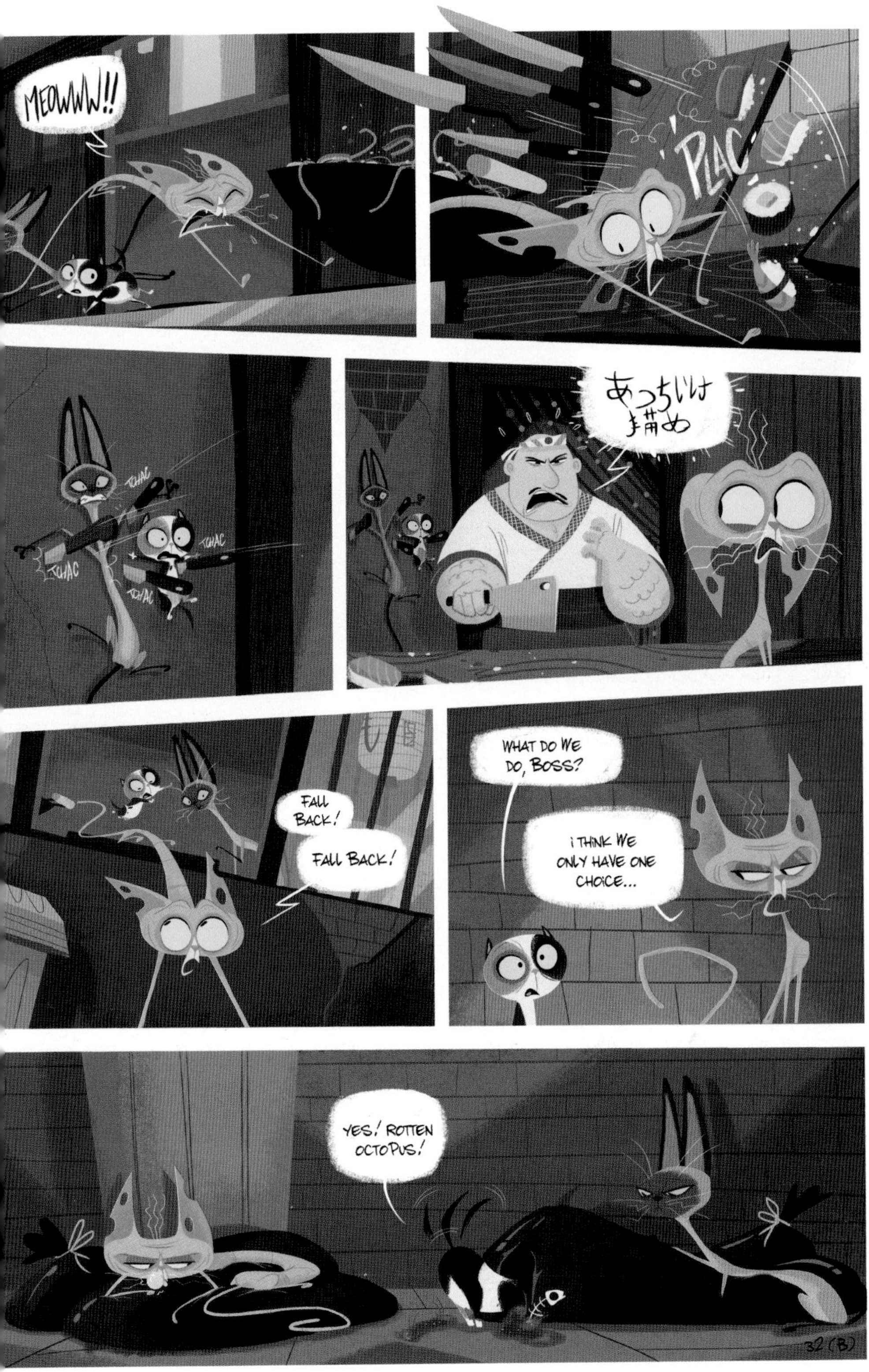
MEOWWW!!
PLAC
TCHAC
TCHAC
TCHAC
TCHAC
あっちいけ
描め
FALL BACK!
FALL BACK!
WHAT DO WE DO, BOSS?
I THINK WE ONLY HAVE ONE CHOICE...
YES! ROTTEN OCTOPUS!
32 (B)

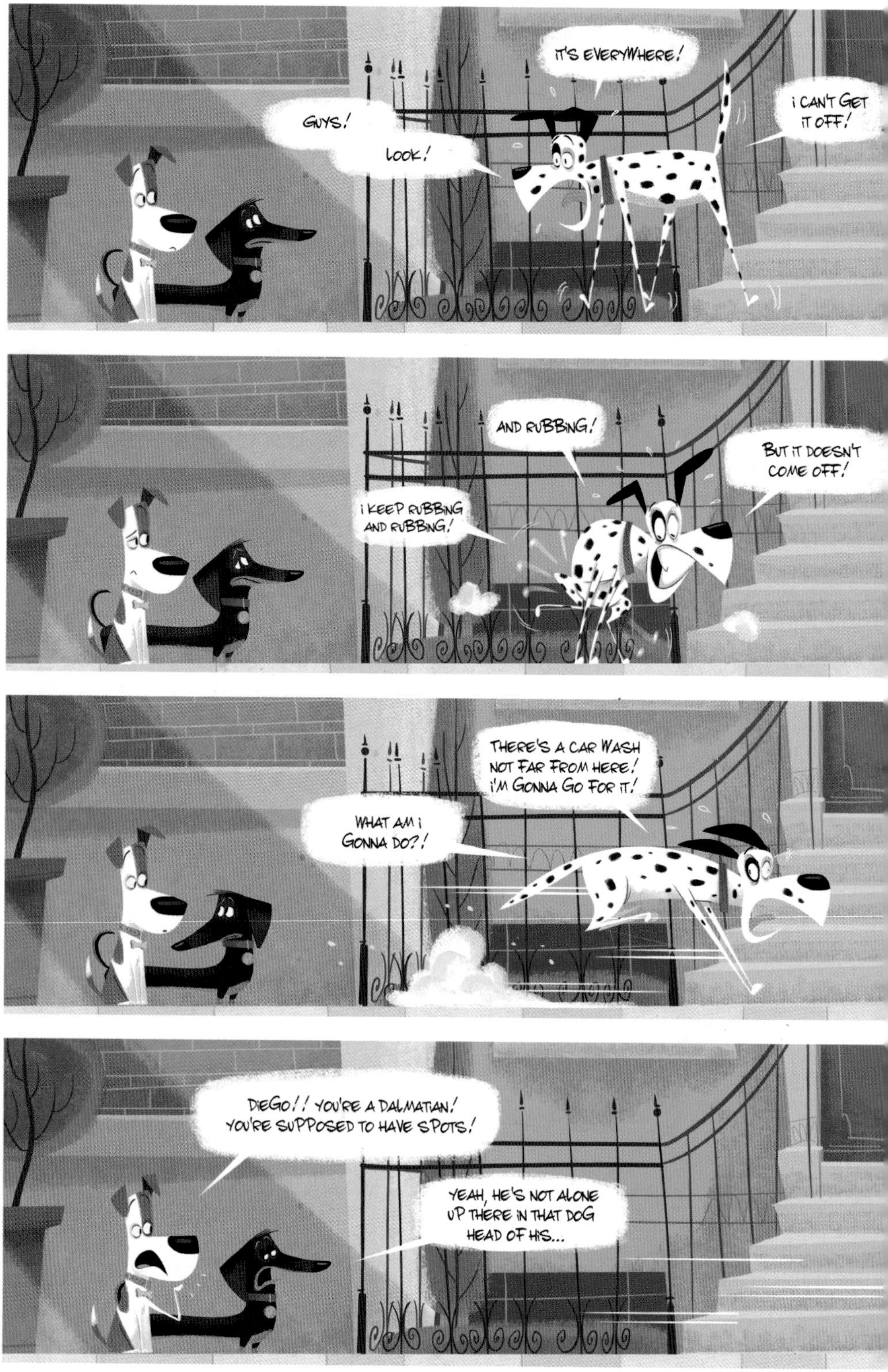
GUYS!
LOOK!
IT'S EVERYWHERE!
I CAN'T GET IT OFF!
I KEEP RUBBING AND RUBBING!
AND RUBBING!
BUT IT DOESN'T COME OFF!
WHAT AM I GONNA DO?!
THERE'S A CAR WASH NOT FAR FROM HERE! I'M GONNA GO FOR IT!
DIEGO!! YOU'RE A DALMATIAN! YOU'RE SUPPOSED TO HAVE SPOTS!
YEAH, HE'S NOT ALONE UP THERE IN THAT DOG HEAD OF HIS...

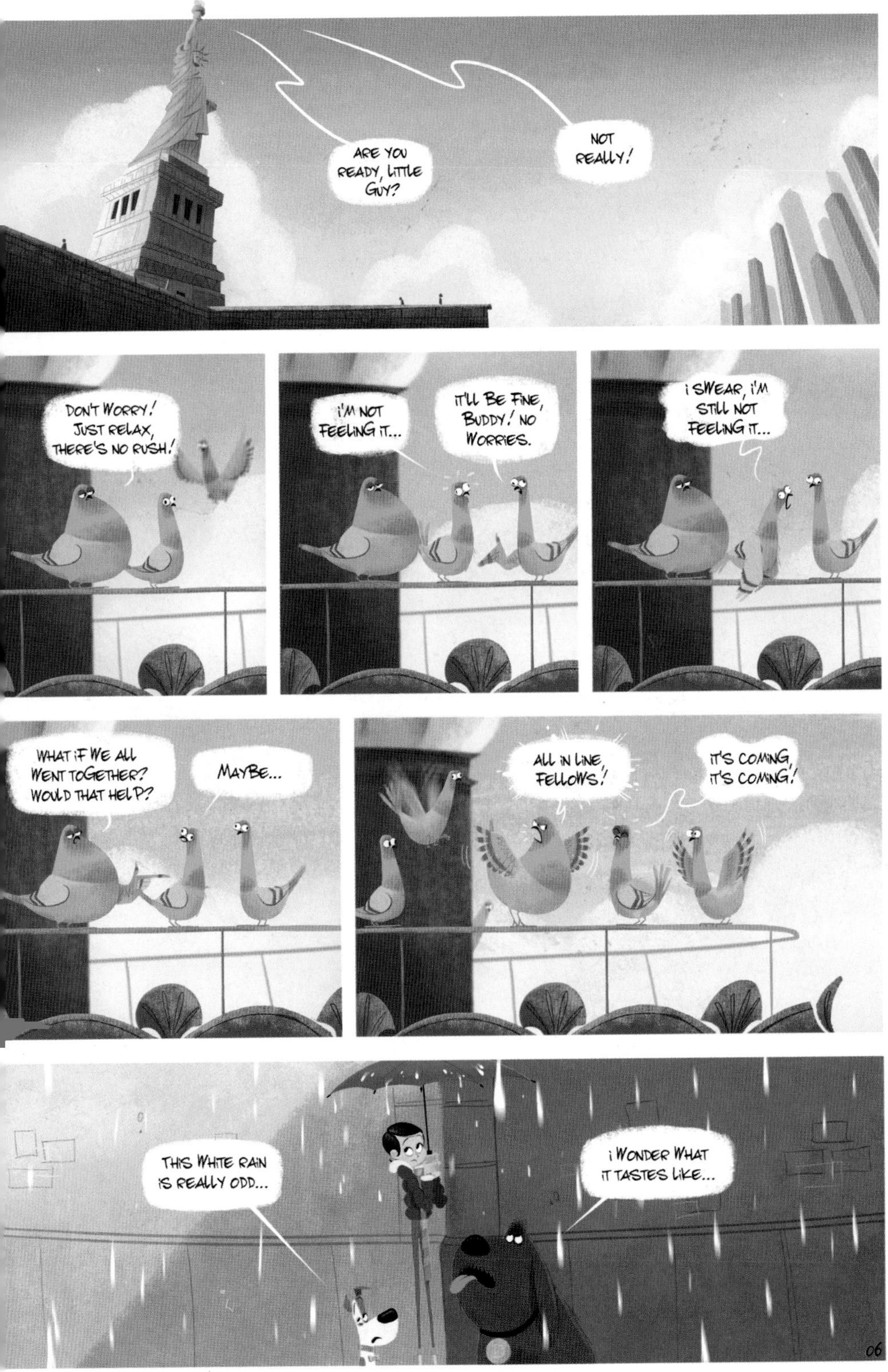
ARE YOU READY, LITTLE GUY?
NOT REALLY!
DON'T WORRY! JUST RELAX, THERE'S NO RUSH!
I'M NOT FEELING IT...
IT'LL BE FINE, BUDDY! NO WORRIES.
I SWEAR, I'M STILL NOT FEELING IT...
WHAT IF WE ALL WENT TOGETHER? WOULD THAT HELP?
MAYBE...
ALL IN LINE, FELLOWS!
IT'S COMING, IT'S COMING!
THIS WHITE RAIN IS REALLY ODD...
I WONDER WHAT IT TASTES LIKE...
06

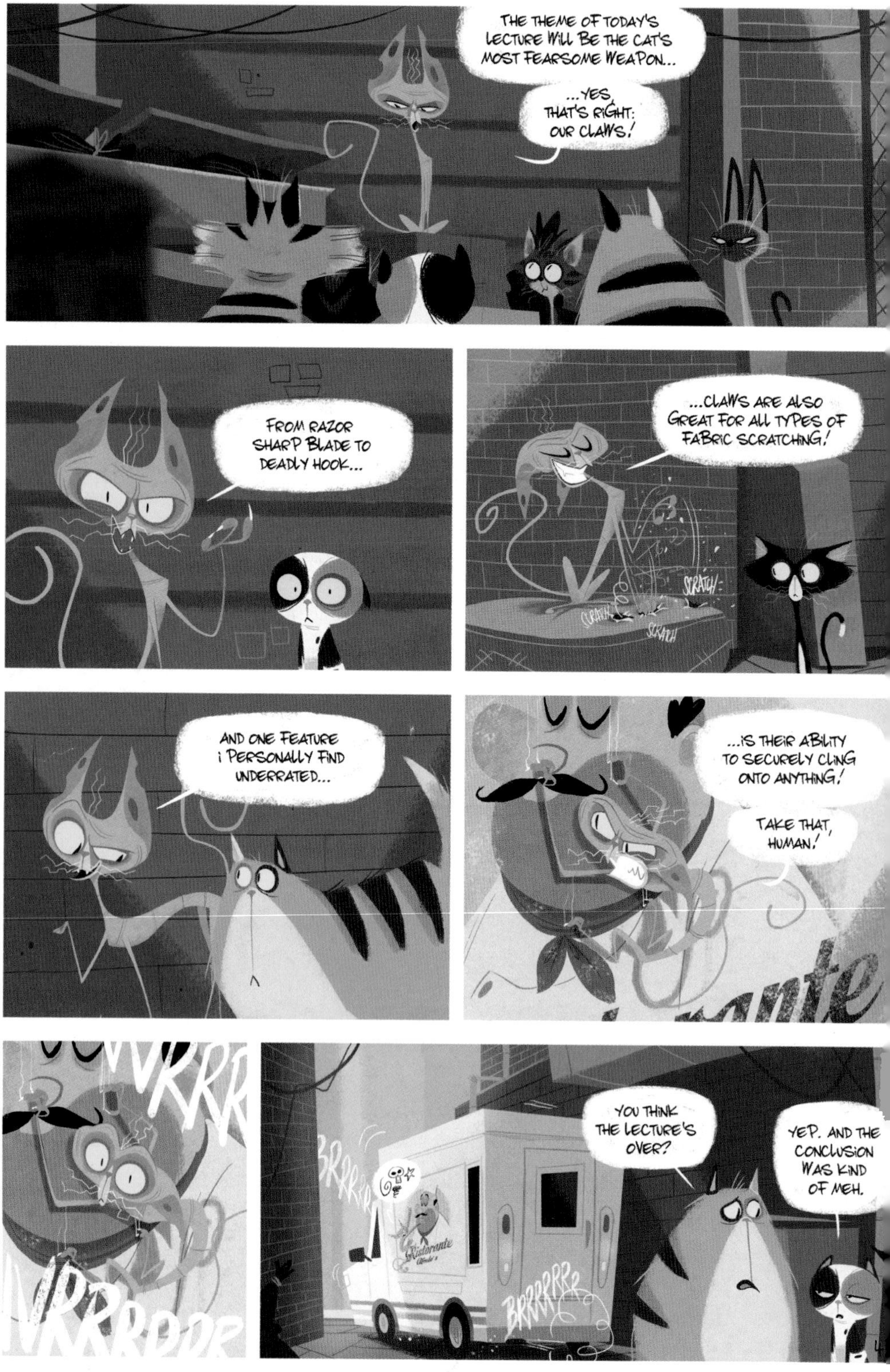
THE THEME OF TODAY'S LECTURE WILL BE THE CAT'S MOST FEARSOME WEAPON...
...YES, THAT'S RIGHT: OUR CLAWS!
FROM RAZOR SHARP BLADE TO DEADLY HOOK...
...CLAWS ARE ALSO GREAT FOR ALL TYPES OF FABRIC SCRATCHING!
SCRATCH
SCRATCH
SCRATCH
AND ONE FEATURE I PERSONALLY FIND UNDERRATED...
...IS THEIR ABILITY TO SECURELY CLING ONTO ANYTHING!
TAKE THAT, HUMAN!
NRRR
NRRRRR
BRRRRR
Ristorante
BRRRRRR
YOU THINK THE LECTURE'S OVER?
YEP. AND THE CONCLUSION WAS KIND OF MEH.

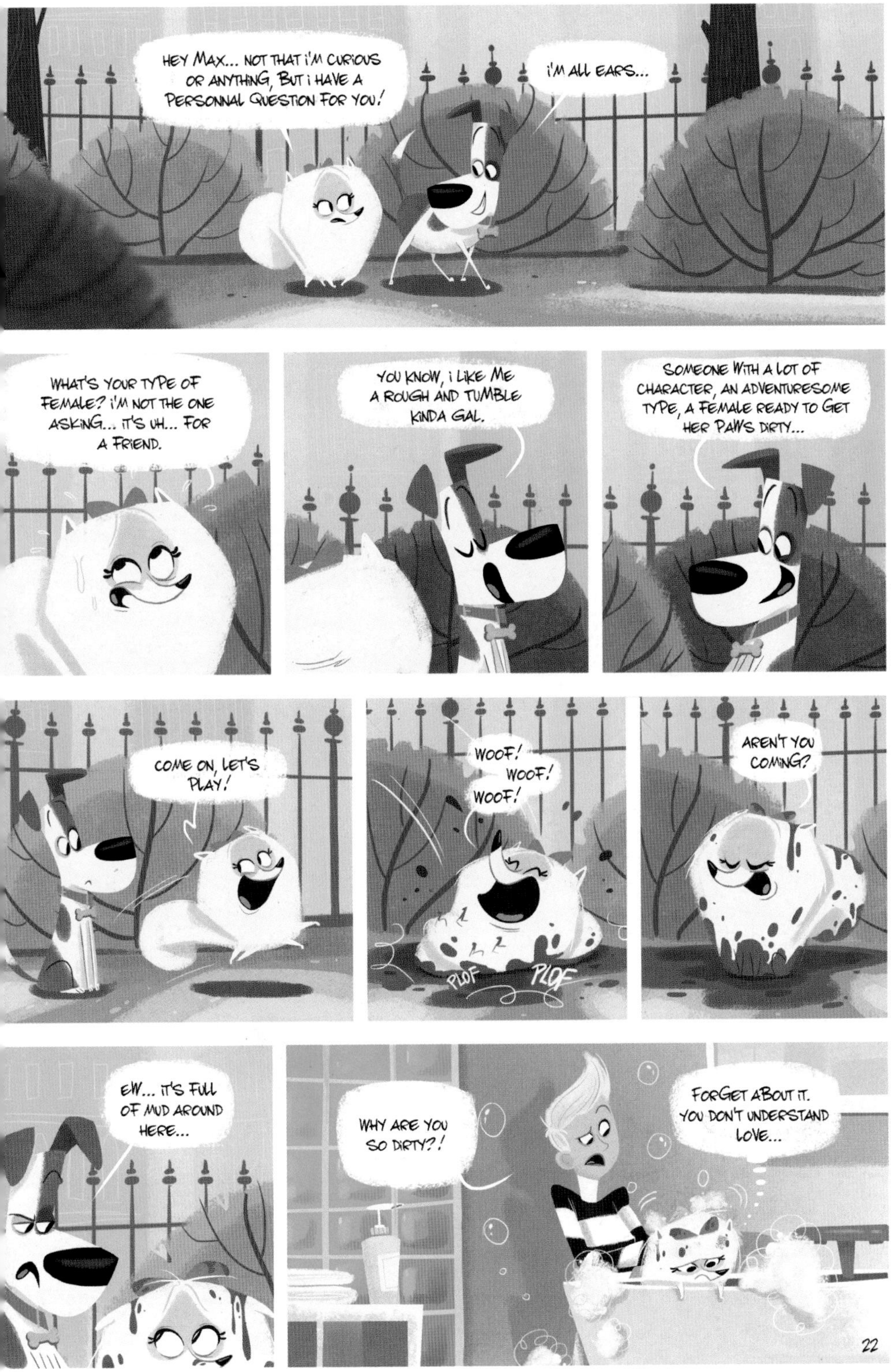

HEY MAX... NOT THAT I'M CURIOUS OR ANYTHING, BUT I HAVE A PERSONNAL QUESTION FOR YOU!
I'M ALL EARS...
WHAT'S YOUR TYPE OF FEMALE? I'M NOT THE ONE ASKING... IT'S UH... FOR A FRIEND.
YOU KNOW, I LIKE ME A ROUGH AND TUMBLE KINDA GAL.
SOMEONE WITH A LOT OF CHARACTER, AN ADVENTURESOME TYPE, A FEMALE READY TO GET HER PAWS DIRTY...
COME ON, LET'S PLAY!
WOOF! WOOF! WOOF!
PLOF PLOF
AREN'T YOU COMING?
EW... IT'S FULL OF MUD AROUND HERE...
WHY ARE YOU SO DIRTY?!
FORGET ABOUT IT. YOU DON'T UNDERSTAND LOVE...
22

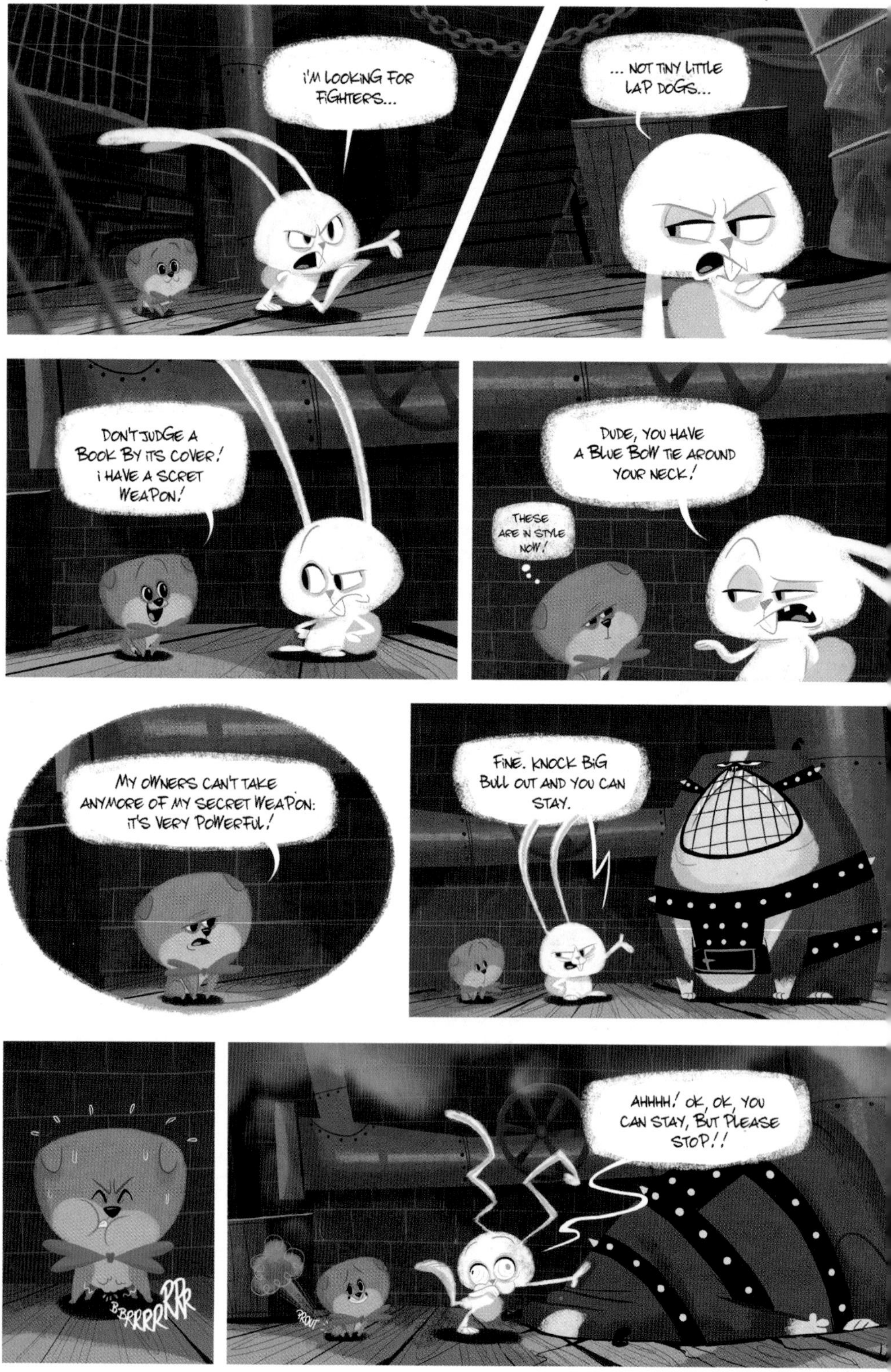
I'M LOOKING FOR FIGHTERS...
... NOT TINY LITTLE LAP DOGS...
DON'T JUDGE A BOOK BY ITS COVER! I HAVE A SCRET WEAPON!
DUDE, YOU HAVE A BLUE BOW TIE AROUND YOUR NECK!
THESE ARE IN STYLE NOW!
MY OWNERS CAN'T TAKE ANYMORE OF MY SECRET WEAPON: IT'S VERY POWERFUL!
FINE. KNOCK BIG BULL OUT AND YOU CAN STAY.
BBRRRRRRR
PROUT
AHHHH! OK, OK, YOU CAN STAY, BUT PLEASE STOP!!

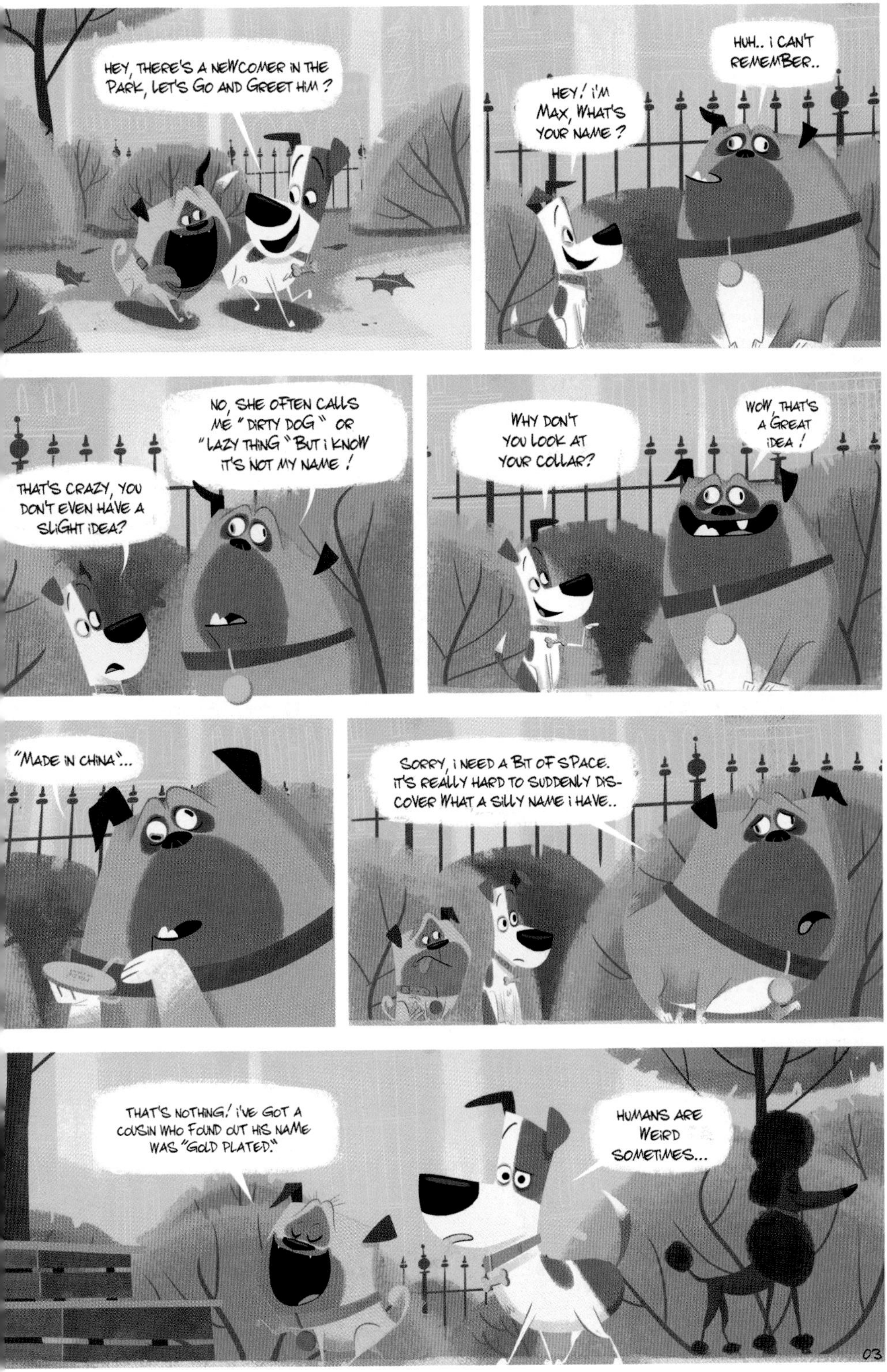
HEY, THERE'S A NEWCOMER IN THE PARK, LET'S GO AND GREET HIM ?
HEY! I'M MAX, WHAT'S YOUR NAME ?
HUH.. I CAN'T REMEMBER..
THAT'S CRAZY, YOU DON'T EVEN HAVE A SLIGHT IDEA?
NO, SHE OFTEN CALLS ME " DIRTY DOG " OR " LAZY THING " BUT I KNOW IT'S NOT MY NAME !
WHY DON'T YOU LOOK AT YOUR COLLAR?
WOW, THAT'S A GREAT IDEA !
"MADE IN CHINA"...
SORRY, I NEED A BIT OF SPACE. IT'S REALLY HARD TO SUDDENLY DIS-COVER WHAT A SILLY NAME I HAVE..
THAT'S NOTHING! I'VE GOT A COUSIN WHO FOUND OUT HIS NAME WAS "GOLD PLATED."
HUMANS ARE WEIRD SOMETIMES...
03

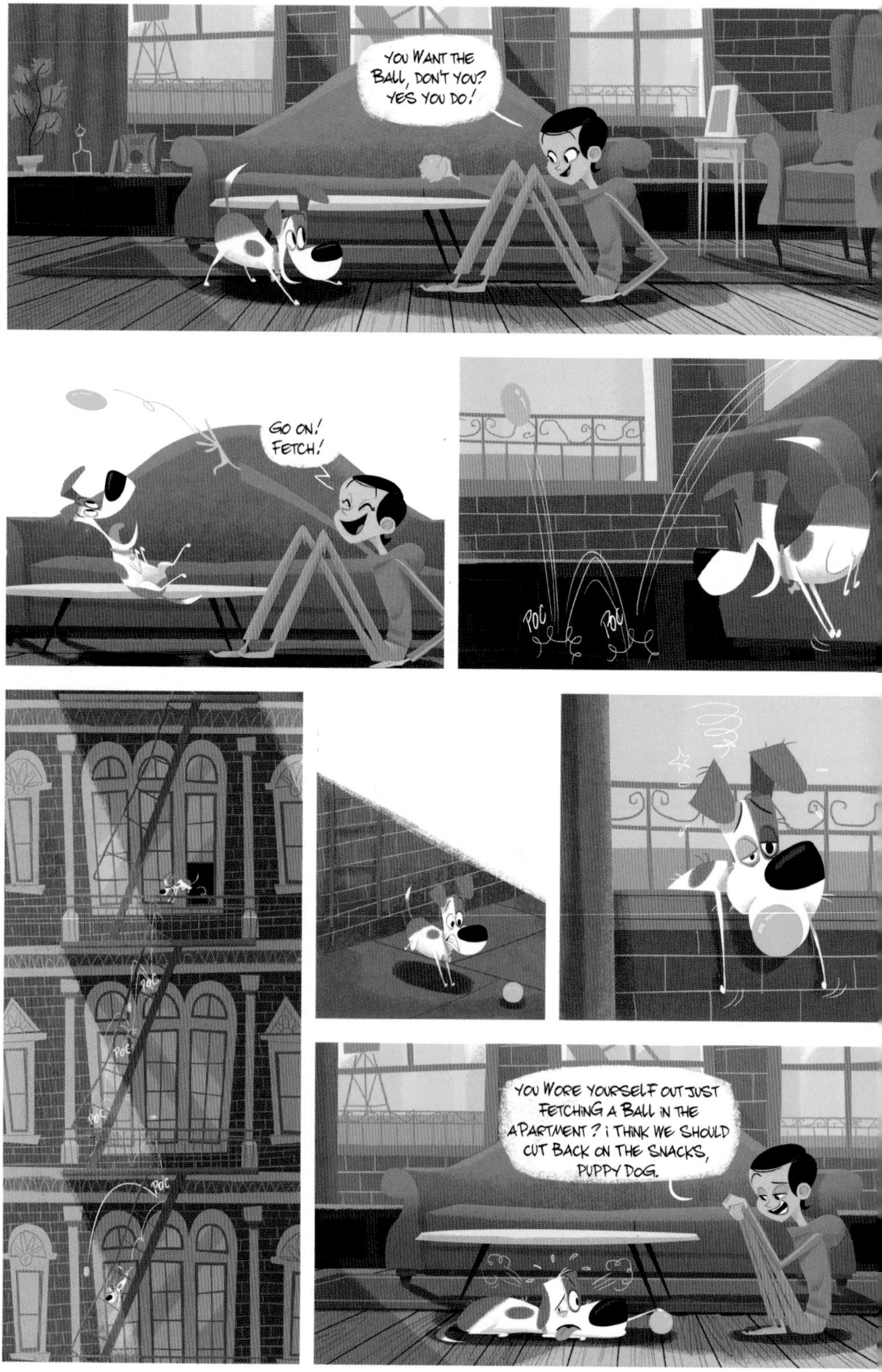

YOU WANT THE BALL, DON'T YOU? YES YOU DO!
GO ON! FETCH!
POC
POC
POC
POC
POC
POC
YOU WORE YOURSELF OUT JUST FETCHING A BALL IN THE APARTMENT? I THINK WE SHOULD CUT BACK ON THE SNACKS, PUPPY DOG.

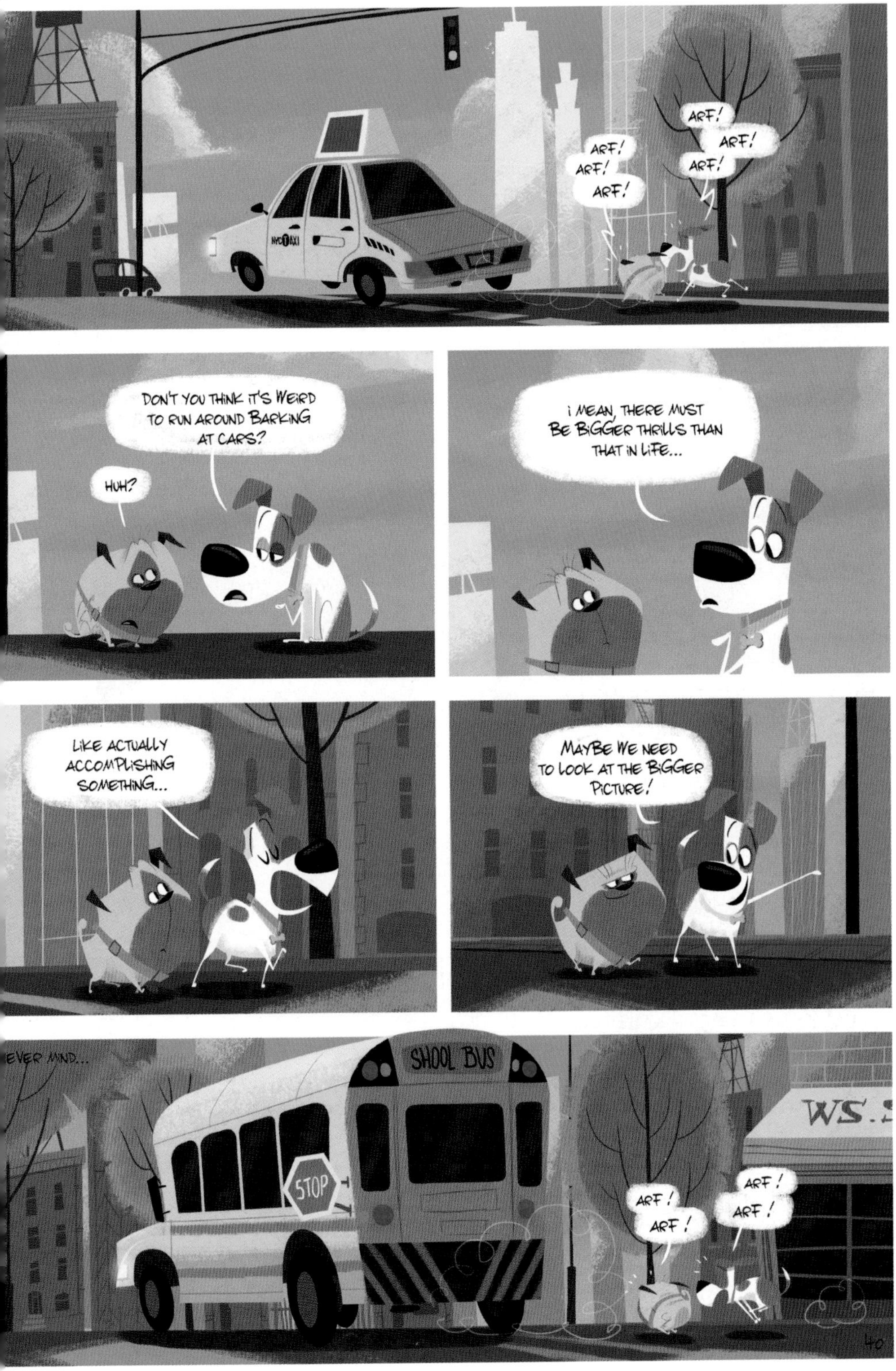
ARF! ARF! ARF!
ARF! ARF! ARF!
DON'T YOU THINK IT'S WEIRD TO RUN AROUND BARKING AT CARS?
HUH?
I MEAN, THERE MUST BE BIGGER THRILLS THAN THAT IN LIFE...
LIKE ACTUALLY ACCOMPLISHING SOMETHING...
MAYBE WE NEED TO LOOK AT THE BIGGER PICTURE!
EVER MIND...
SHOOL BUS
STOP
ARF! ARF!
ARF! ARF!

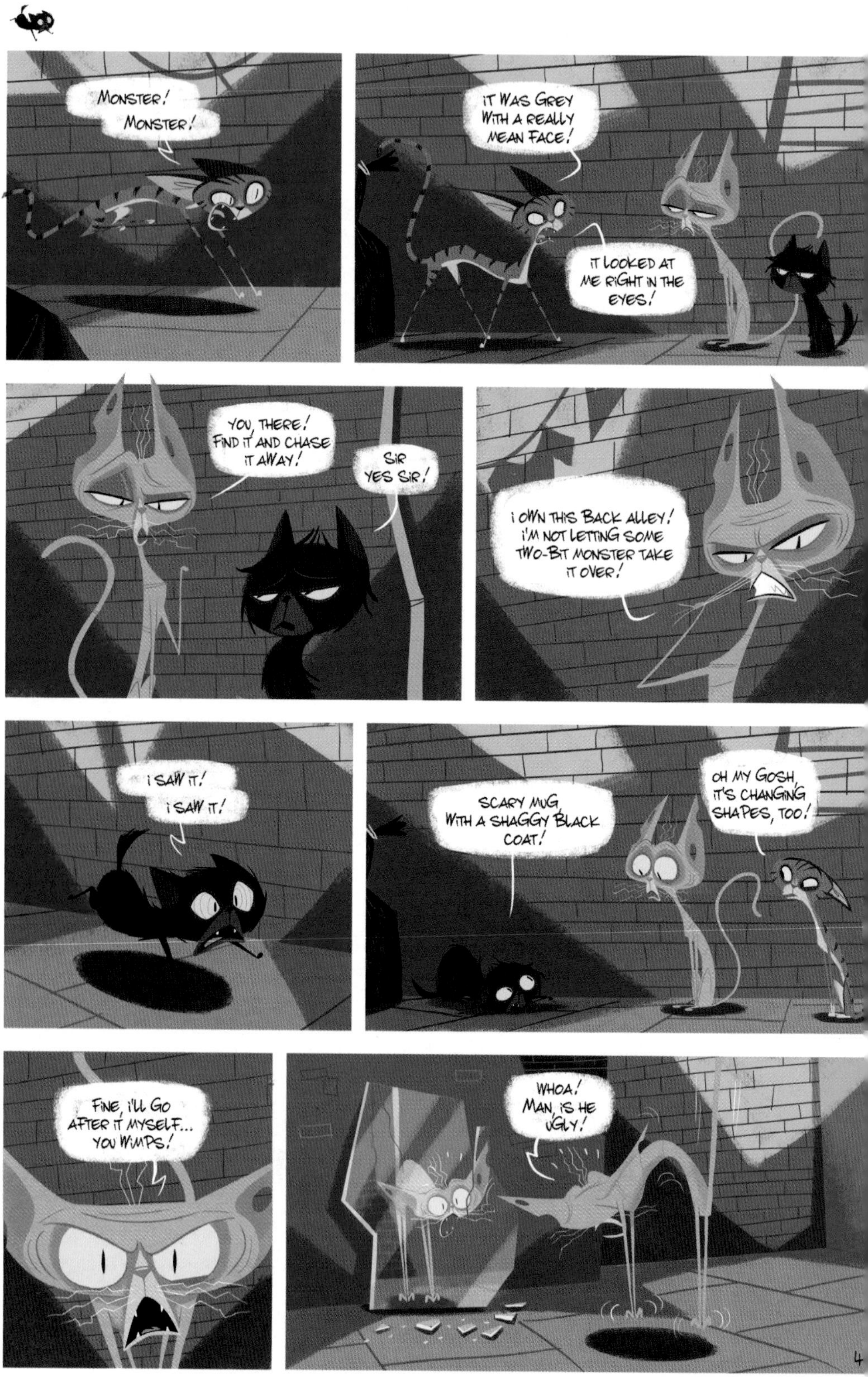
MONSTER!
MONSTER!
IT WAS GREY WITH A REALLY MEAN FACE!
IT LOOKED AT ME RIGHT IN THE EYES!
YOU, THERE! FIND IT AND CHASE IT AWAY!
SIR YES SIR!
I OWN THIS BACK ALLEY! I'M NOT LETTING SOME TWO-BIT MONSTER TAKE IT OVER!
I SAW IT!
I SAW IT!
SCARY MUG, WITH A SHAGGY BLACK COAT!
OH MY GOSH, IT'S CHANGING SHAPES, TOO!
FINE, I'LL GO AFTER IT MYSELF... YOU WIMPS!
WHOA! MAN, IS HE UGLY!

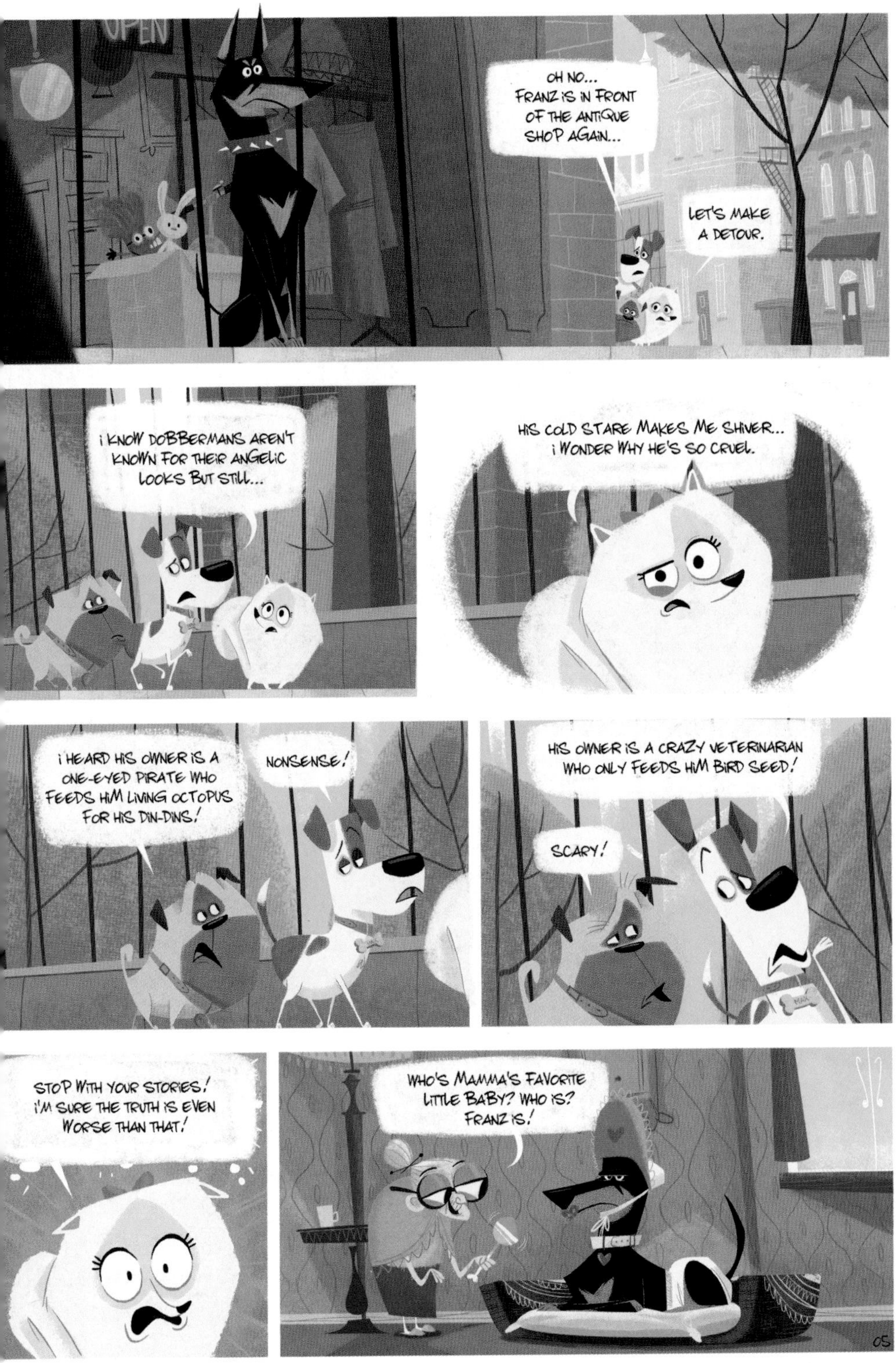

OPEN
OH NO... FRANZ IS IN FRONT OF THE ANTIQUE SHOP AGAIN...
LET'S MAKE A DETOUR.
I KNOW DOBBERMANS AREN'T KNOWN FOR THEIR ANGELIC LOOKS BUT STILL...
HIS COLD STARE MAKES ME SHIVER... I WONDER WHY HE'S SO CRUEL.
I HEARD HIS OWNER IS A ONE-EYED PIRATE WHO FEEDS HIM LIVING OCTOPUS FOR HIS DIN-DINS!
NONSENSE!
HIS OWNER IS A CRAZY VETERINARIAN WHO ONLY FEEDS HIM BIRD SEED!
SCARY!
STOP WITH YOUR STORIES! I'M SURE THE TRUTH IS EVEN WORSE THAN THAT!
WHO'S MAMMA'S FAVORITE LITTLE BABY? WHO IS? FRANZ IS!
05

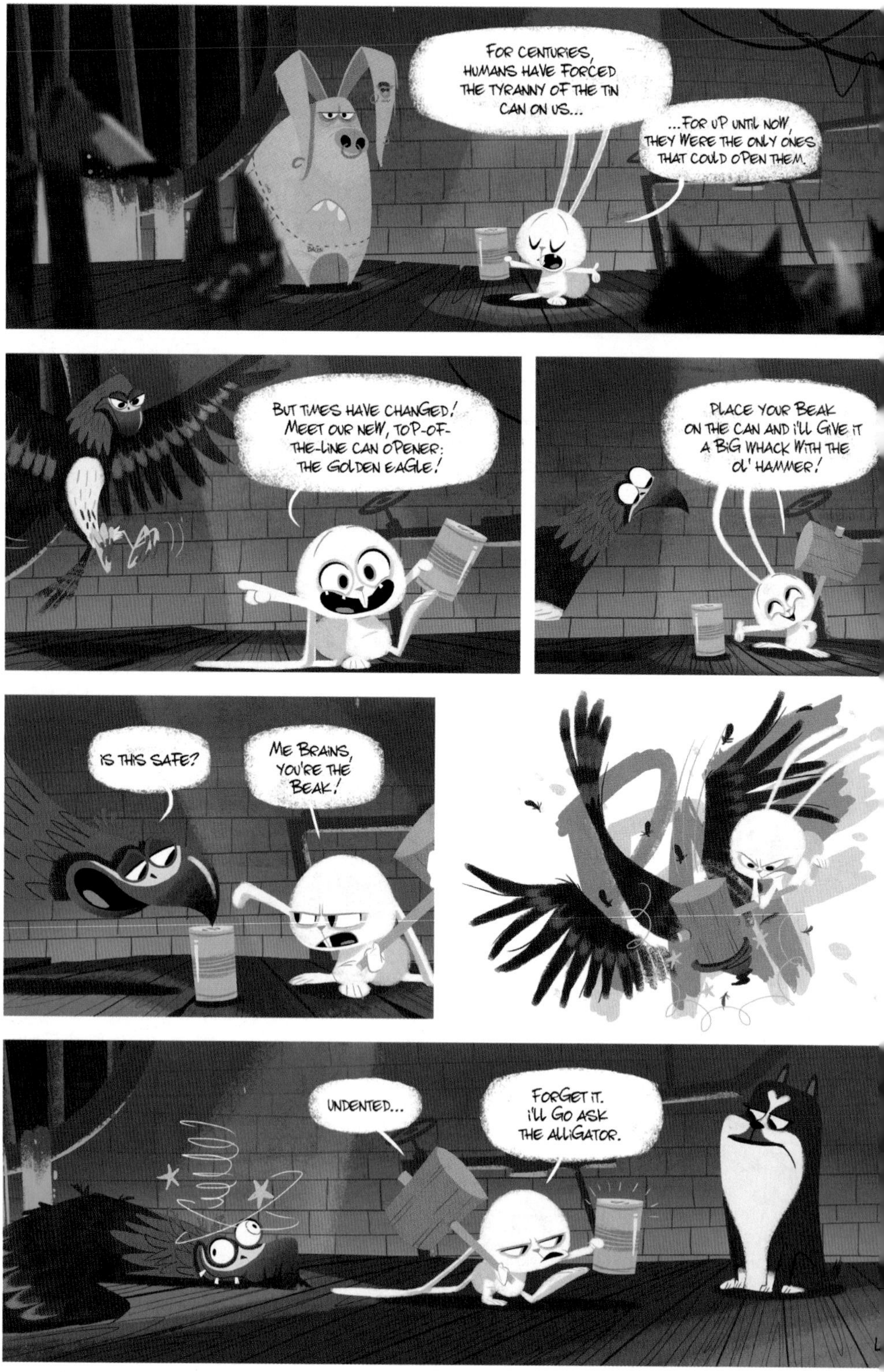
FOR CENTURIES, HUMANS HAVE FORCED THE TYRANNY OF THE TIN CAN ON US...
...FOR UP UNTIL NOW, THEY WERE THE ONLY ONES THAT COULD OPEN THEM.
BUT TIMES HAVE CHANGED! MEET OUR NEW, TOP-OF-THE-LINE CAN OPENER: THE GOLDEN EAGLE!
PLACE YOUR BEAK ON THE CAN AND I'LL GIVE IT A BIG WHACK WITH THE OL' HAMMER!
IS THIS SAFE?
ME BRAINS, YOU'RE THE BEAK!
UNDENTED...
FORGET IT. I'LL GO ASK THE ALLIGATOR.

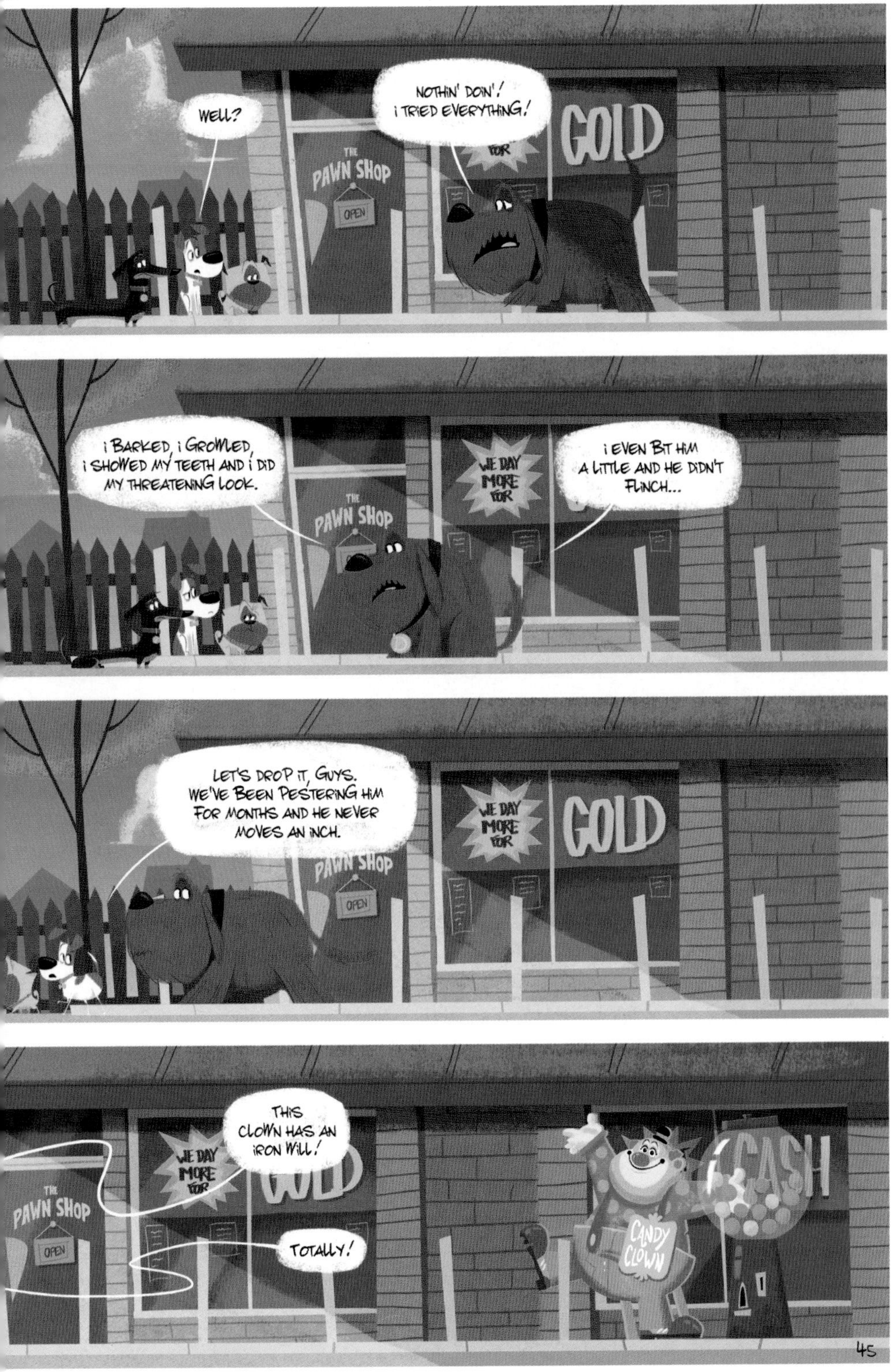
WELL?
NOTHIN' DOIN'! I TRIED EVERYTHING!
THE PAWN SHOP
OPEN
GOLD
I BARKED, I GROWLED, I SHOWED MY TEETH AND I DID MY THREATENING LOOK.
I EVEN BIT HIM A LITTLE AND HE DIDN'T FLINCH...
LET'S DROP IT, GUYS. WE'VE BEEN PESTERING HIM FOR MONTHS AND HE NEVER MOVES AN INCH.
THIS CLOWN HAS AN IRON WILL!
TOTALLY!
CASH
CANDY CLOWN
45

HAVE THEY GONE? CAN I COME IN?

YEAH, HURRY UP! IT'S GONNA START!

I'M SO HAPPY WE GET TO WATCH MY FAVORITE SERIES TOGETHER...

I'M ONLY DOING THIS FOR YOU, YOU KNOW. THIS KIND OF THING BORES ME.

YOU JUST WAIT! YOU WON'T FALL ASLEEP DURING THIS TREASURE...

IT STARTS IN 5 MINUTES. JUST ENOUGH TIME FOR ME TO SUMMARIZE WHAT'S HAPPENING SO YOU'RE NOT LOST...

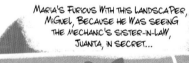

MARIA'S FURIOUS WITH THIS LANDSCAPER, MIGUEL, BECAUSE HE WAS SEEING THE MECHANIC'S SISTER-IN-LAW, JUANITA, IN SECRET...

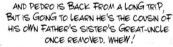

AND PEDRO IS BACK FROM A LONG TRIP, BUT IS GOING TO LEARN HE'S THE COUSIN OF HIS OWN FATHER'S SISTER'S GREAT-UNCLE ONCE REMOVED. WHEW!

BUT...

HEY!

AT LEAST YOU DIDN'T FALL ASLEEP DURING THE SHOW...

BOUNDER...

La Pasión de la Pasión

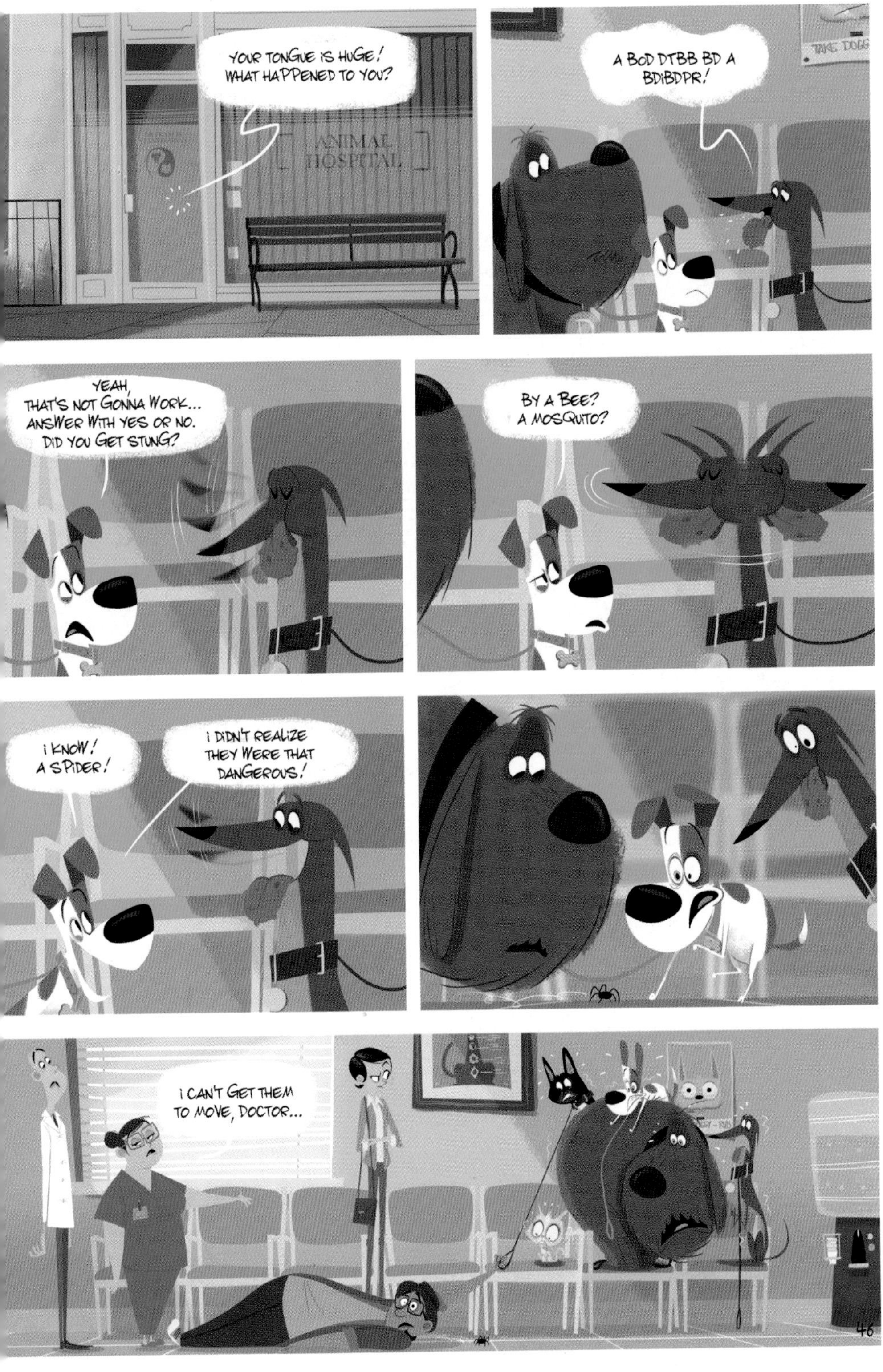
ANIMAL HOSPITAL
YOUR TONGUE IS HUGE! WHAT HAPPENED TO YOU?
TAKE DOGG
A BOD DTBB BD A BDIBDPR!
YEAH, THAT'S NOT GONNA WORK... ANSWER WITH YES OR NO. DID YOU GET STUNG?
BY A BEE? A MOSQUITO?
I KNOW! A SPIDER!
I DIDN'T REALIZE THEY WERE THAT DANGEROUS!
I CAN'T GET THEM TO MOVE, DOCTOR...
46

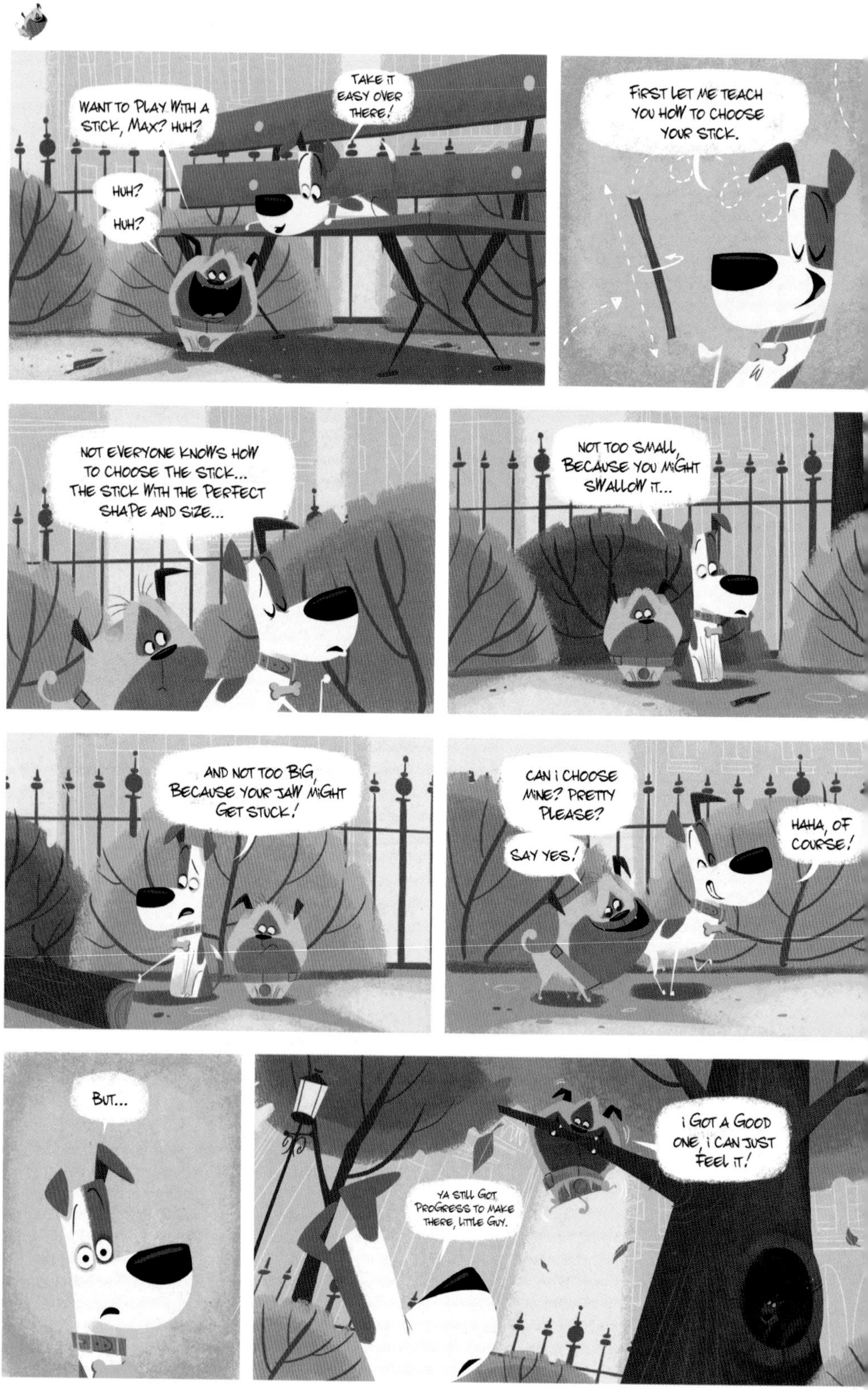

WANT TO PLAY WITH A STICK, MAX? HUH?
HUH?
HUH?
TAKE IT EASY OVER THERE!
FIRST LET ME TEACH YOU HOW TO CHOOSE YOUR STICK.
NOT EVERYONE KNOWS HOW TO CHOOSE THE STICK... THE STICK WITH THE PERFECT SHAPE AND SIZE...
NOT TOO SMALL, BECAUSE YOU MIGHT SWALLOW IT...
AND NOT TOO BIG, BECAUSE YOUR JAW MIGHT GET STUCK!
CAN I CHOOSE MINE? PRETTY PLEASE?
SAY YES!
HAHA, OF COURSE!
BUT...
I GOT A GOOD ONE, I CAN JUST FEEL IT!
YA STILL GOT PROGRESS TO MAKE THERE, LITTLE GUY.

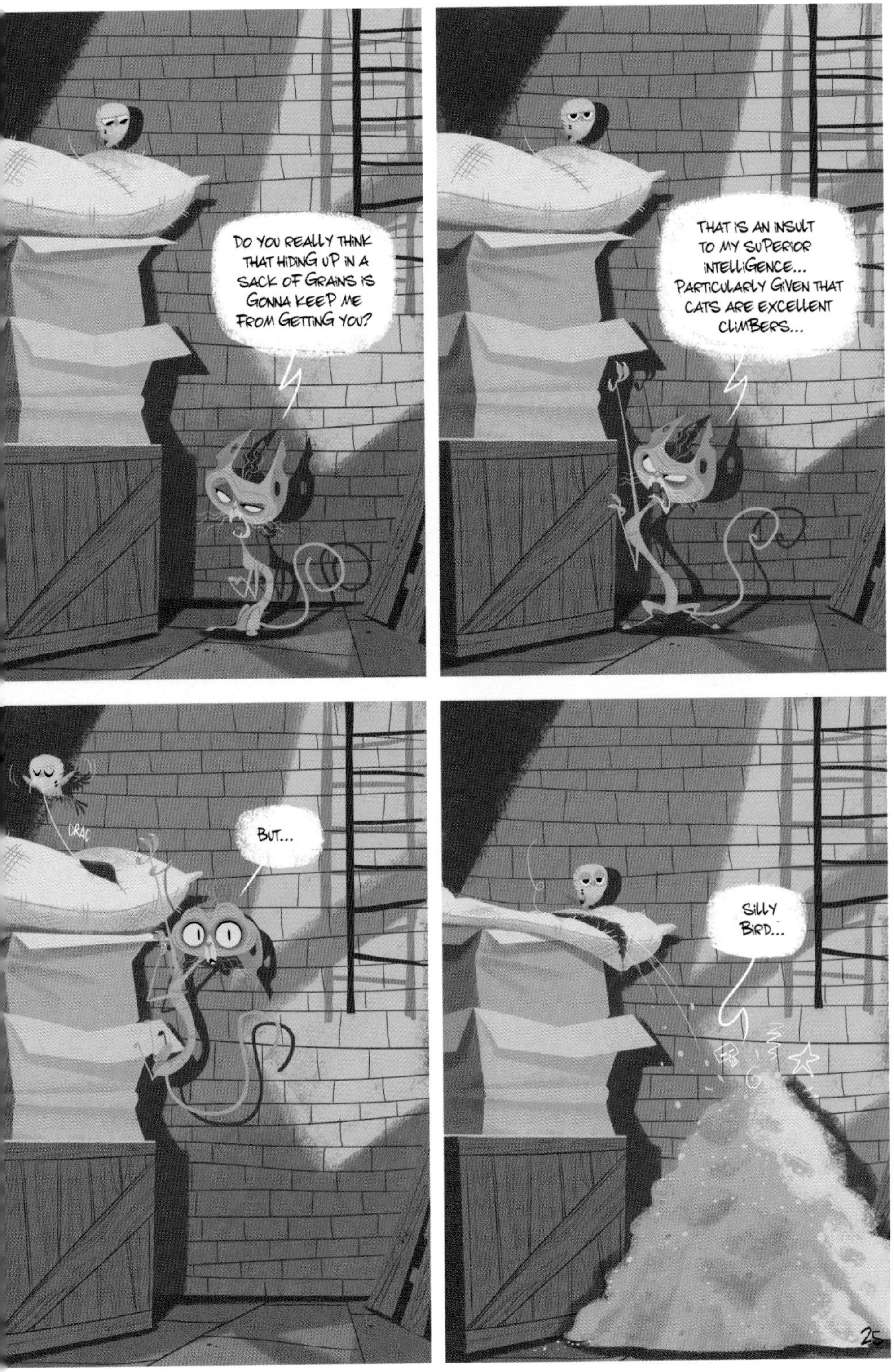
DO YOU REALLY THINK THAT HIDING UP IN A SACK OF GRAINS IS GONNA KEEP ME FROM GETTING YOU?
THAT IS AN INSULT TO MY SUPERIOR INTELLIGENCE... PARTICULARLY GIVEN THAT CATS ARE EXCELLENT CLIMBERS...
CRAC
BUT...
SILLY BIRD...
25

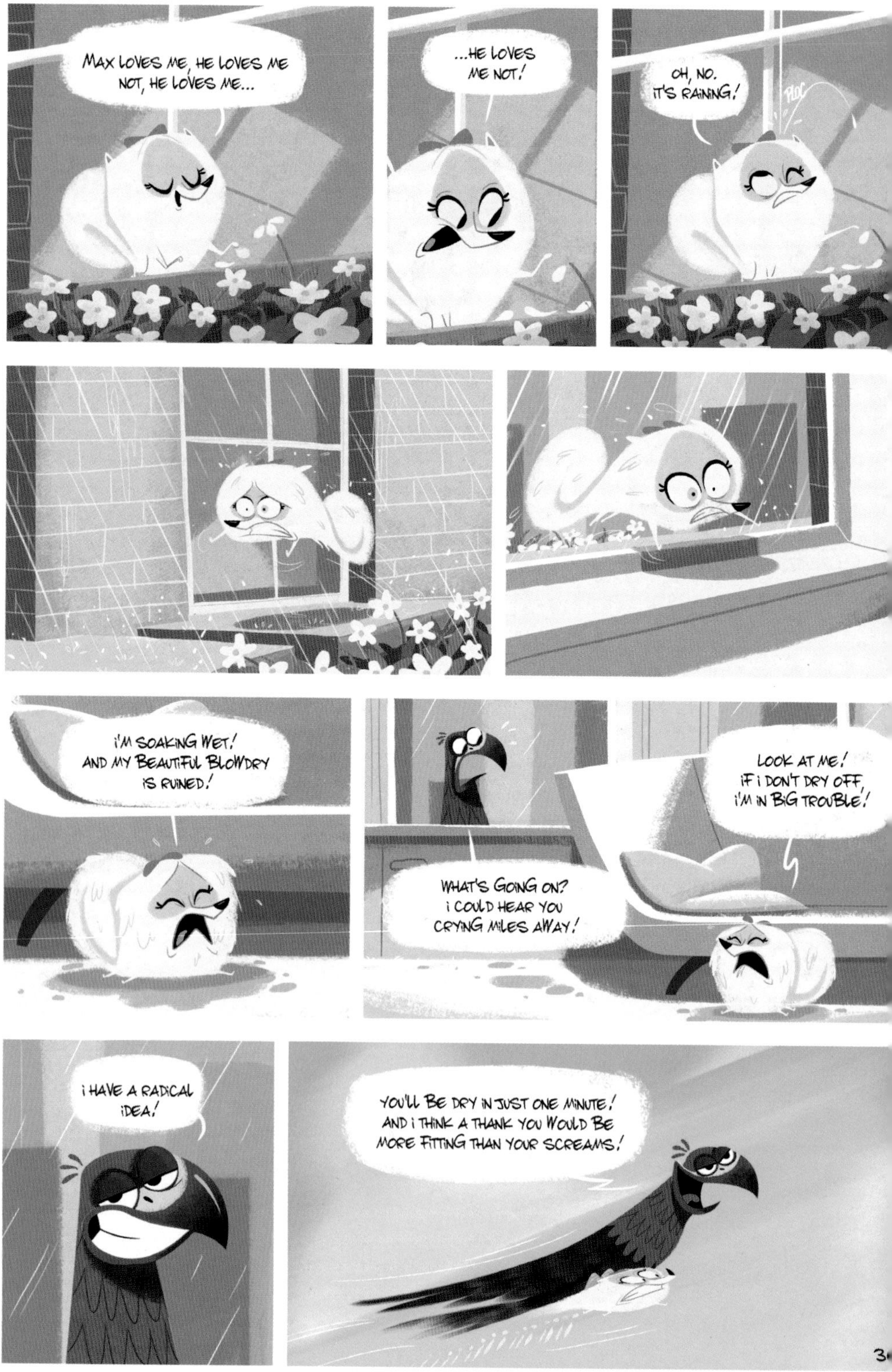
MAX LOVES ME, HE LOVES ME NOT, HE LOVES ME...
...HE LOVES ME NOT!
OH, NO. IT'S RAINING!
PLOC
I'M SOAKING WET! AND MY BEAUTIFUL BLOWDRY IS RUINED!
LOOK AT ME! IF I DON'T DRY OFF, I'M IN BIG TROUBLE!
WHAT'S GOING ON? I COULD HEAR YOU CRYING MILES AWAY!
I HAVE A RADICAL IDEA!
YOU'LL BE DRY IN JUST ONE MINUTE! AND I THINK A THANK YOU WOULD BE MORE FITTING THAN YOUR SCREAMS!

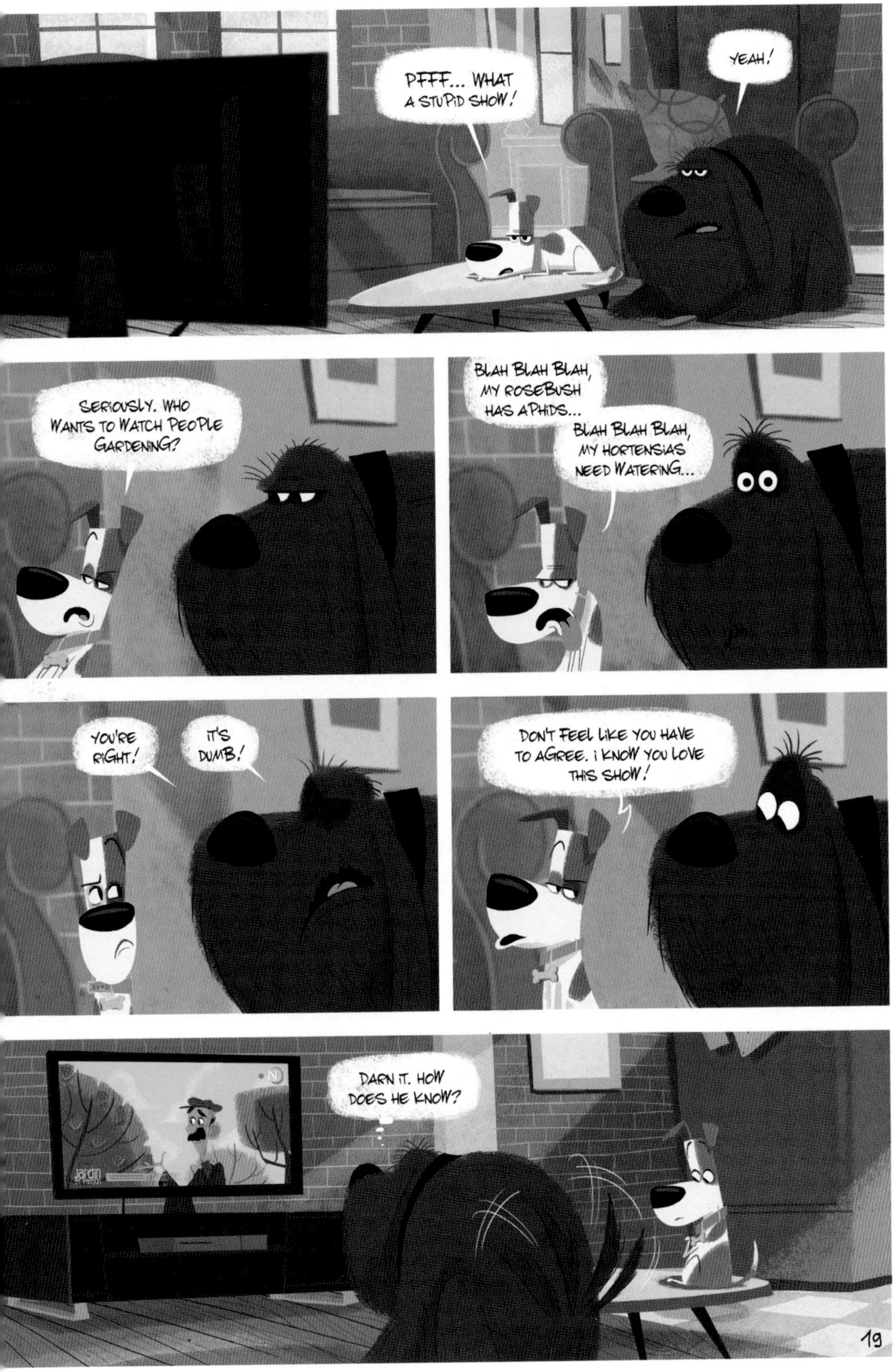
PFFF... WHAT A STUPID SHOW!
YEAH!
SERIOUSLY. WHO WANTS TO WATCH PEOPLE GARDENING?
BLAH BLAH BLAH, MY ROSEBUSH HAS APHIDS...
BLAH BLAH BLAH, MY HORTENSIAS NEED WATERING...
YOU'RE RIGHT!
IT'S DUMB!
DON'T FEEL LIKE YOU HAVE TO AGREE. I KNOW YOU LOVE THIS SHOW!
DARN IT. HOW DOES HE KNOW?
19

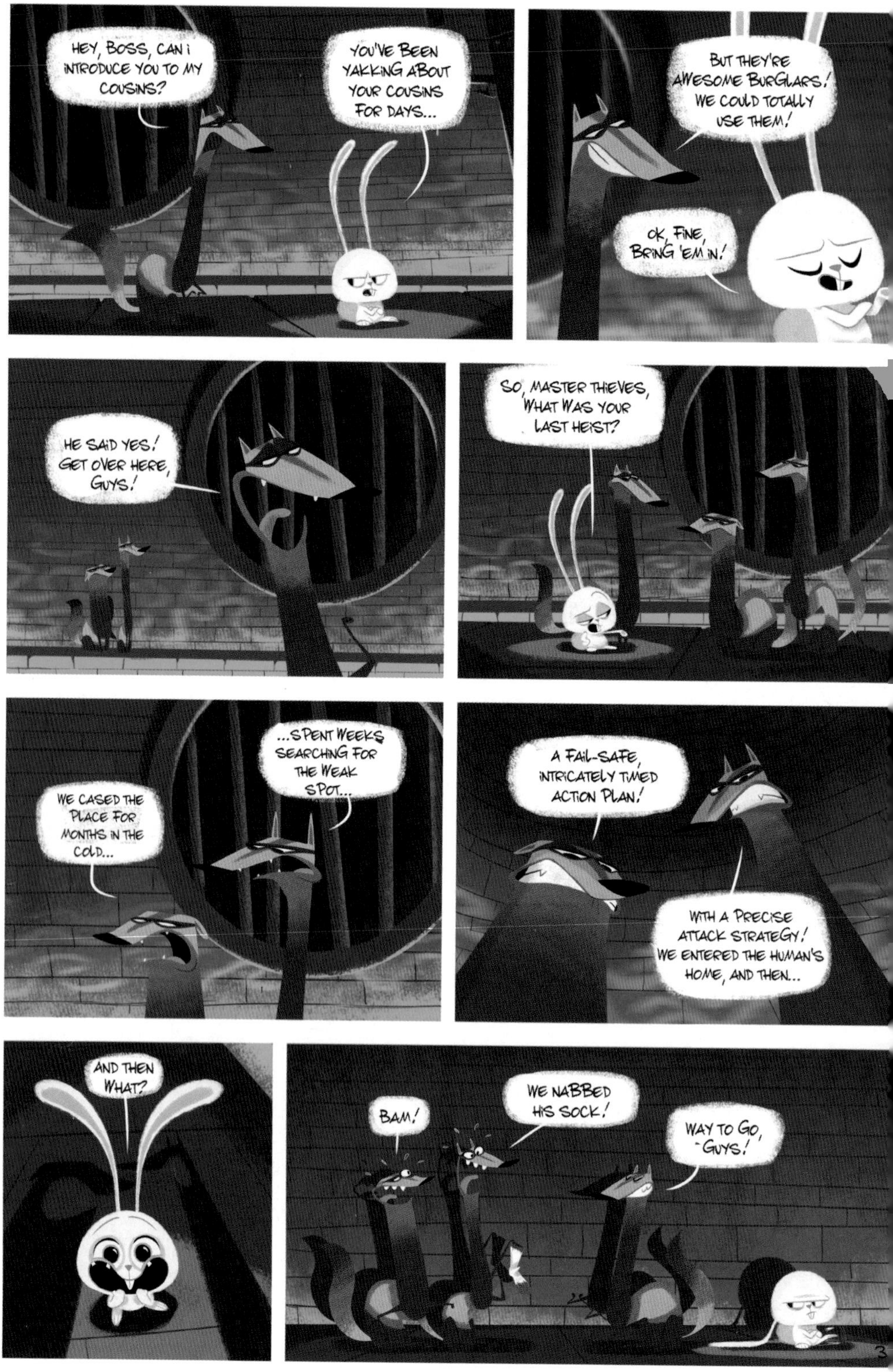

HEY, BOSS, CAN I INTRODUCE YOU TO MY COUSINS?
YOU'VE BEEN YAKKING ABOUT YOUR COUSINS FOR DAYS...
BUT THEY'RE AWESOME BURGLARS! WE COULD TOTALLY USE THEM!
OK, FINE, BRING 'EM IN!
HE SAID YES! GET OVER HERE, GUYS!
SO, MASTER THIEVES, WHAT WAS YOUR LAST HEIST?
WE CASED THE PLACE FOR MONTHS IN THE COLD...
...SPENT WEEKS SEARCHING FOR THE WEAK SPOT...
A FAIL-SAFE, INTRICATELY TIMED ACTION PLAN!
WITH A PRECISE ATTACK STRATEGY! WE ENTERED THE HUMAN'S HOME, AND THEN...
AND THEN WHAT?
BAM!
WE NABBED HIS SOCK!
WAY TO GO, GUYS!

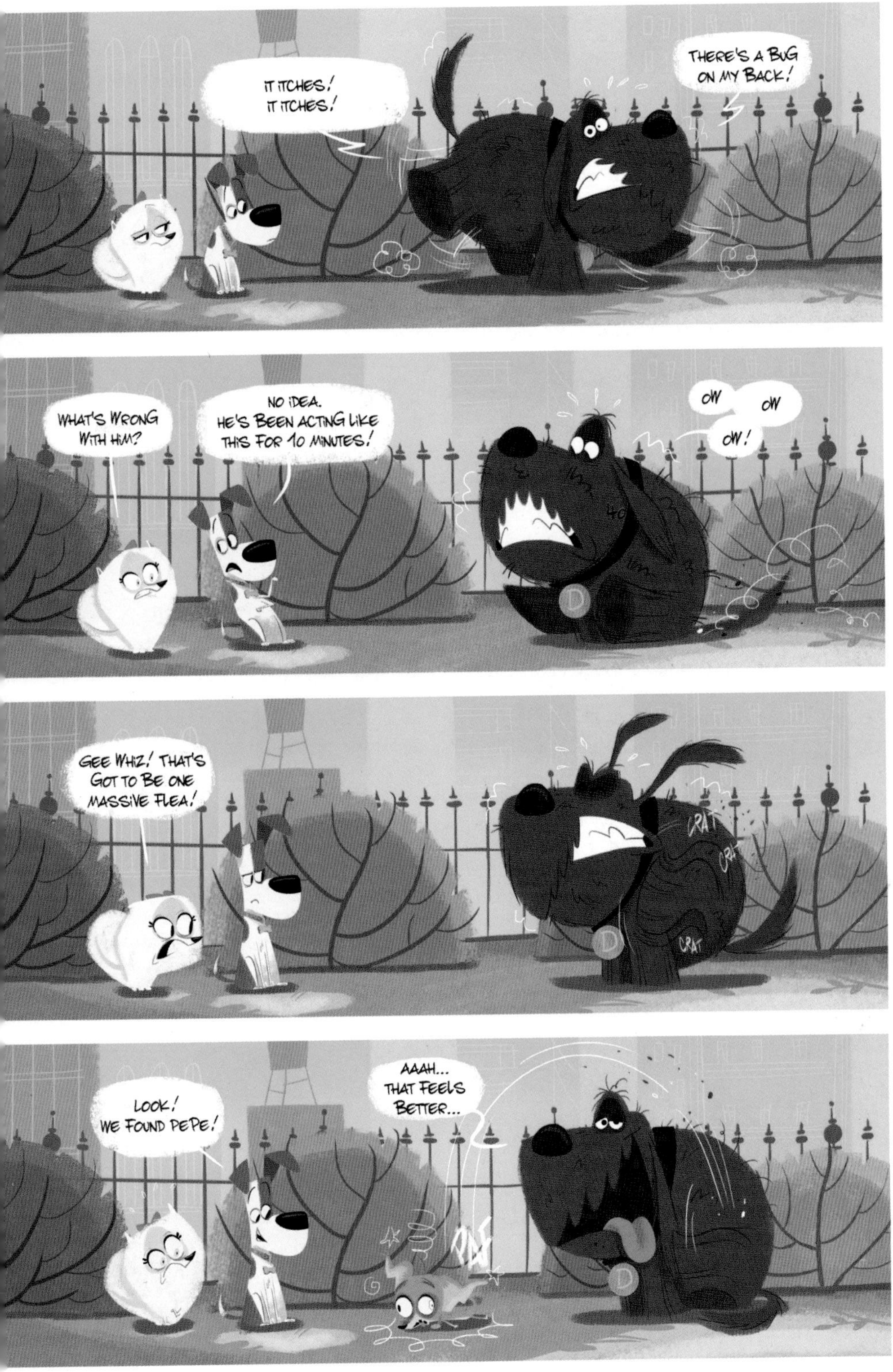
IT ITCHES!
IT ITCHES!
THERE'S A BUG ON MY BACK!
WHAT'S WRONG WITH HIM?
NO IDEA. HE'S BEEN ACTING LIKE THIS FOR 10 MINUTES!
OW
OW
OW!
GEE WHIZ! THAT'S GOT TO BE ONE MASSIVE FLEA!
CRAT
CRAT
CRAT
LOOK! WE FOUND PEPE!
AAAH... THAT FEELS BETTER...

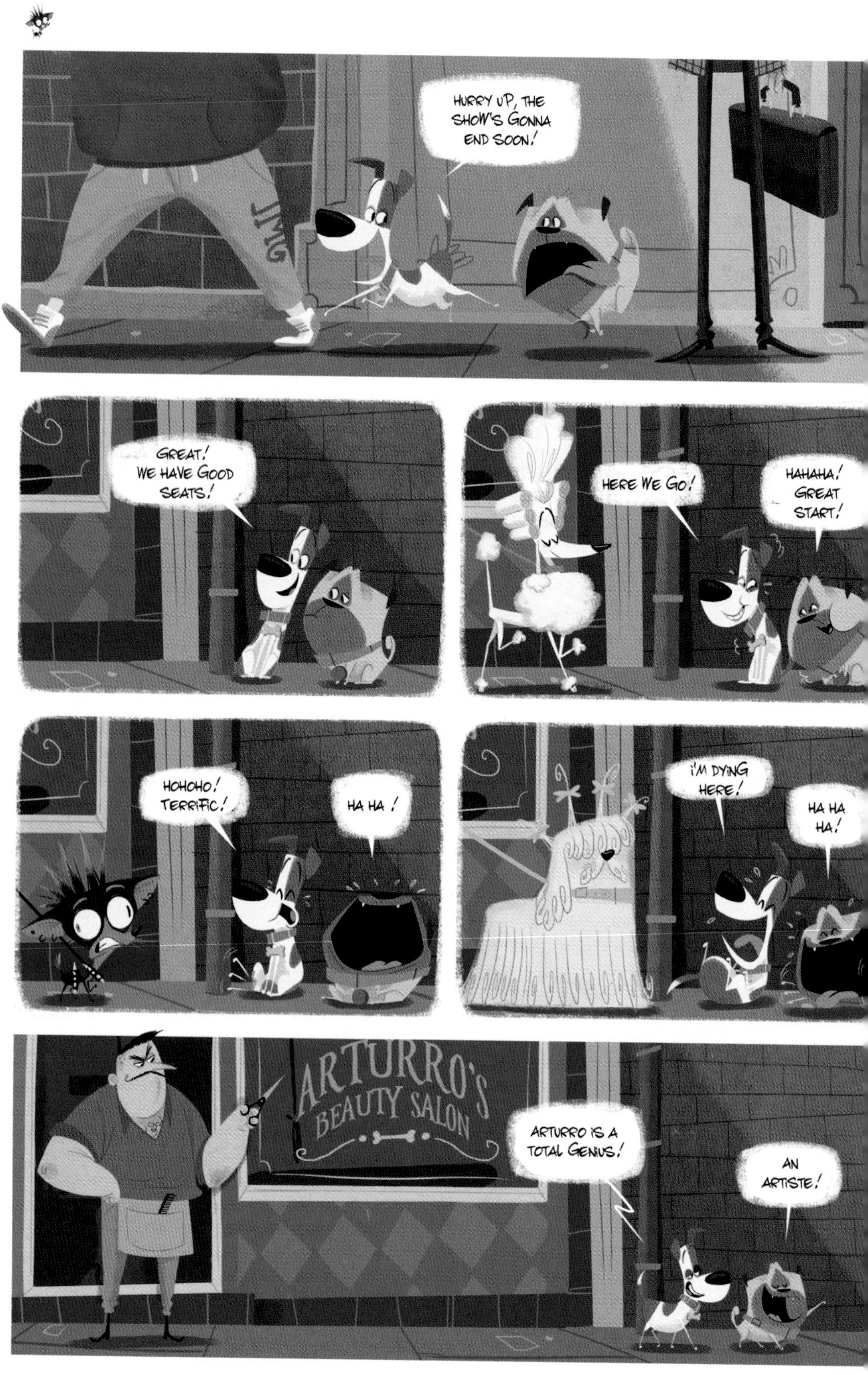
HURRY UP, THE SHOW'S GONNA END SOON!
GREAT! WE HAVE GOOD SEATS!
HERE WE GO!
HAHAHA! GREAT START!
HOHOHO! TERRIFIC!
HA HA!
I'M DYING HERE!
HA HA HA!
ARTURRO'S BEAUTY SALON
ARTURRO IS A TOTAL GENIUS!
AN ARTISTE!

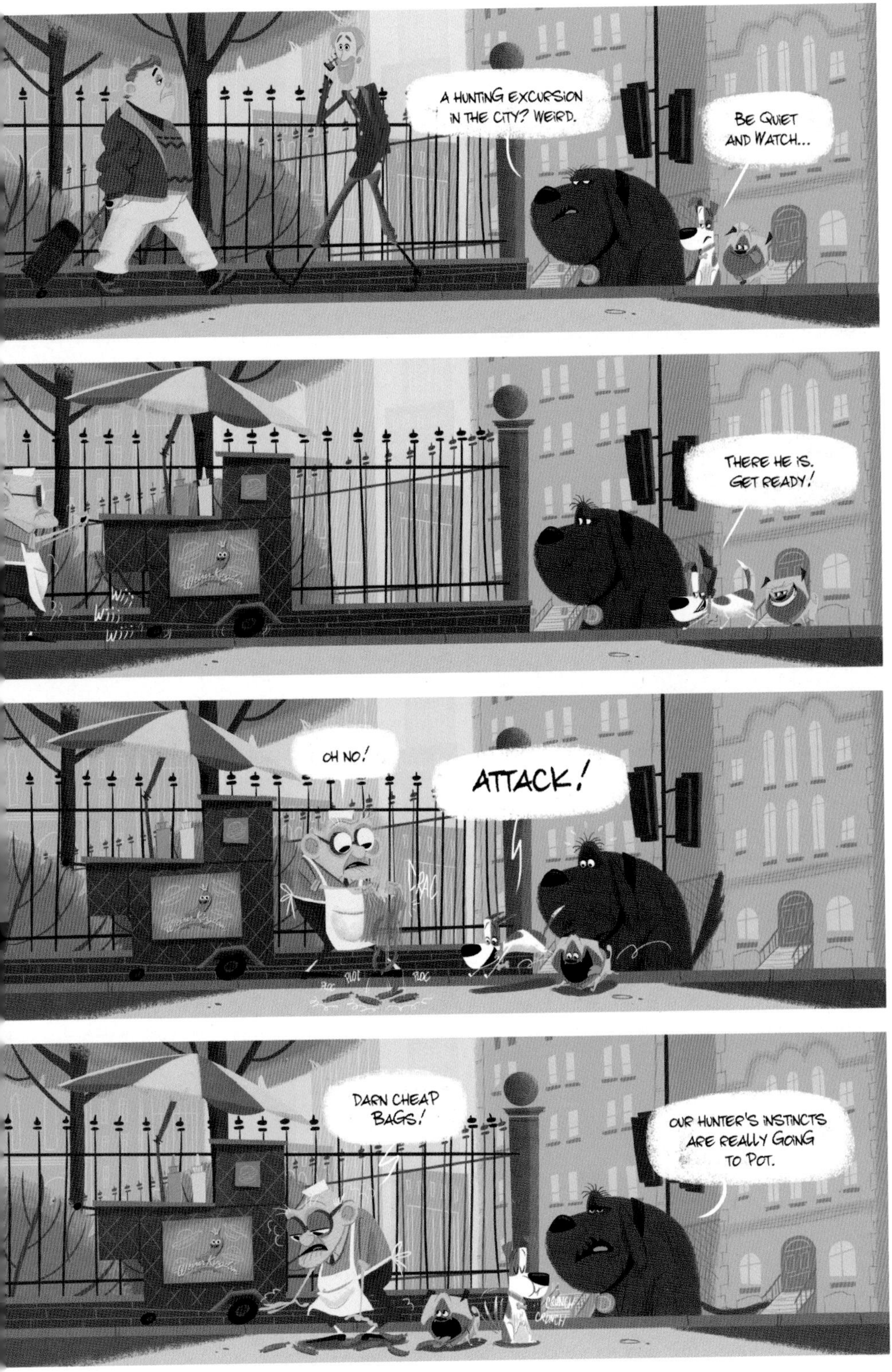
A HUNTING EXCURSION IN THE CITY? WEIRD.
BE QUIET AND WATCH...
THERE HE IS. GET READY!
OH NO!
ATTACK!
DARN CHEAP BAGS!
OUR HUNTER'S INSTINCTS ARE REALLY GOING TO POT.

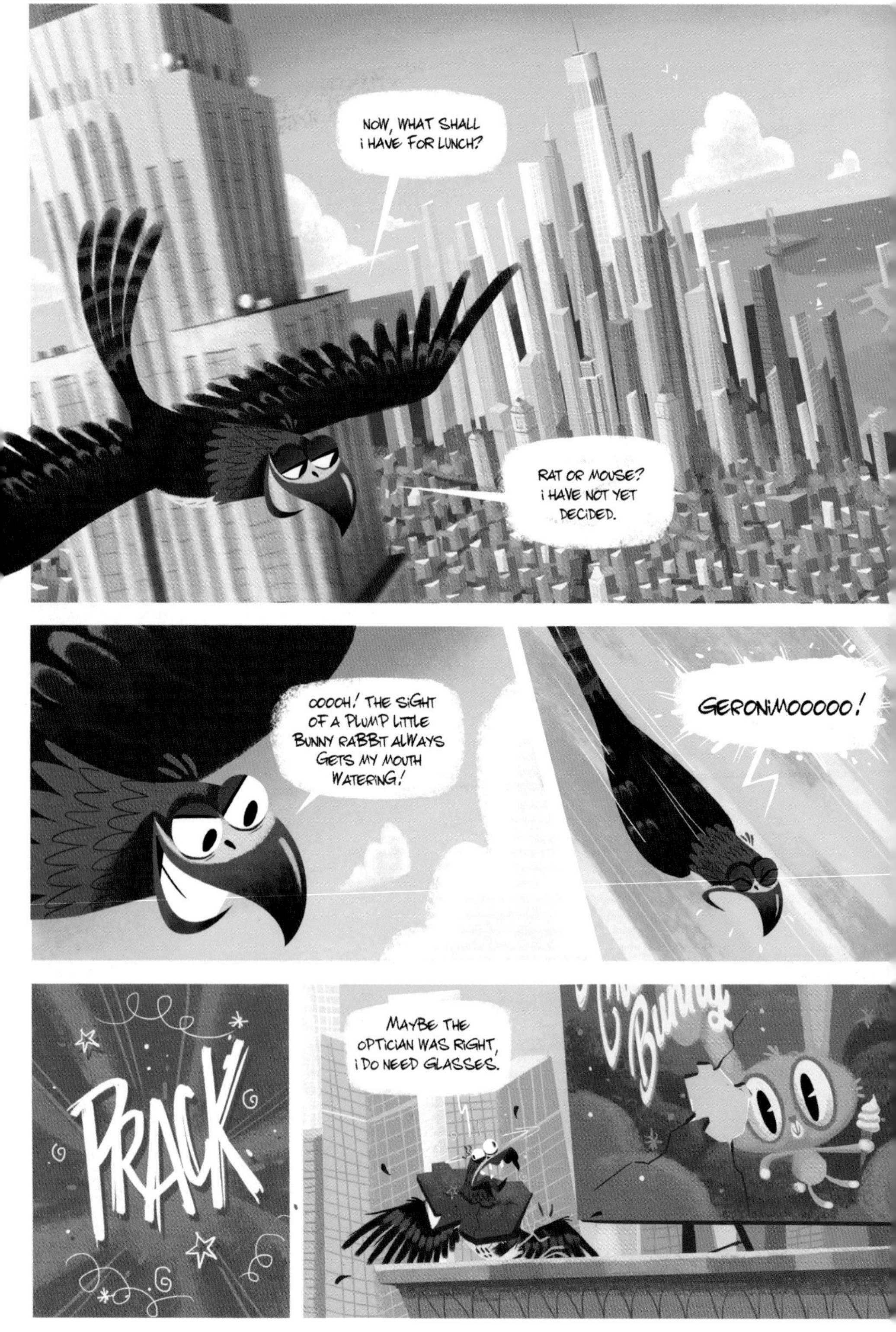
NOW, WHAT SHALL I HAVE FOR LUNCH?
RAT OR MOUSE? I HAVE NOT YET DECIDED.
OOOOH! THE SIGHT OF A PLUMP LITTLE BUNNY RABBIT ALWAYS GETS MY MOUTH WATERING!
GERONIMOOOOO!
PRACK
MAYBE THE OPTICIAN WAS RIGHT, I DO NEED GLASSES.

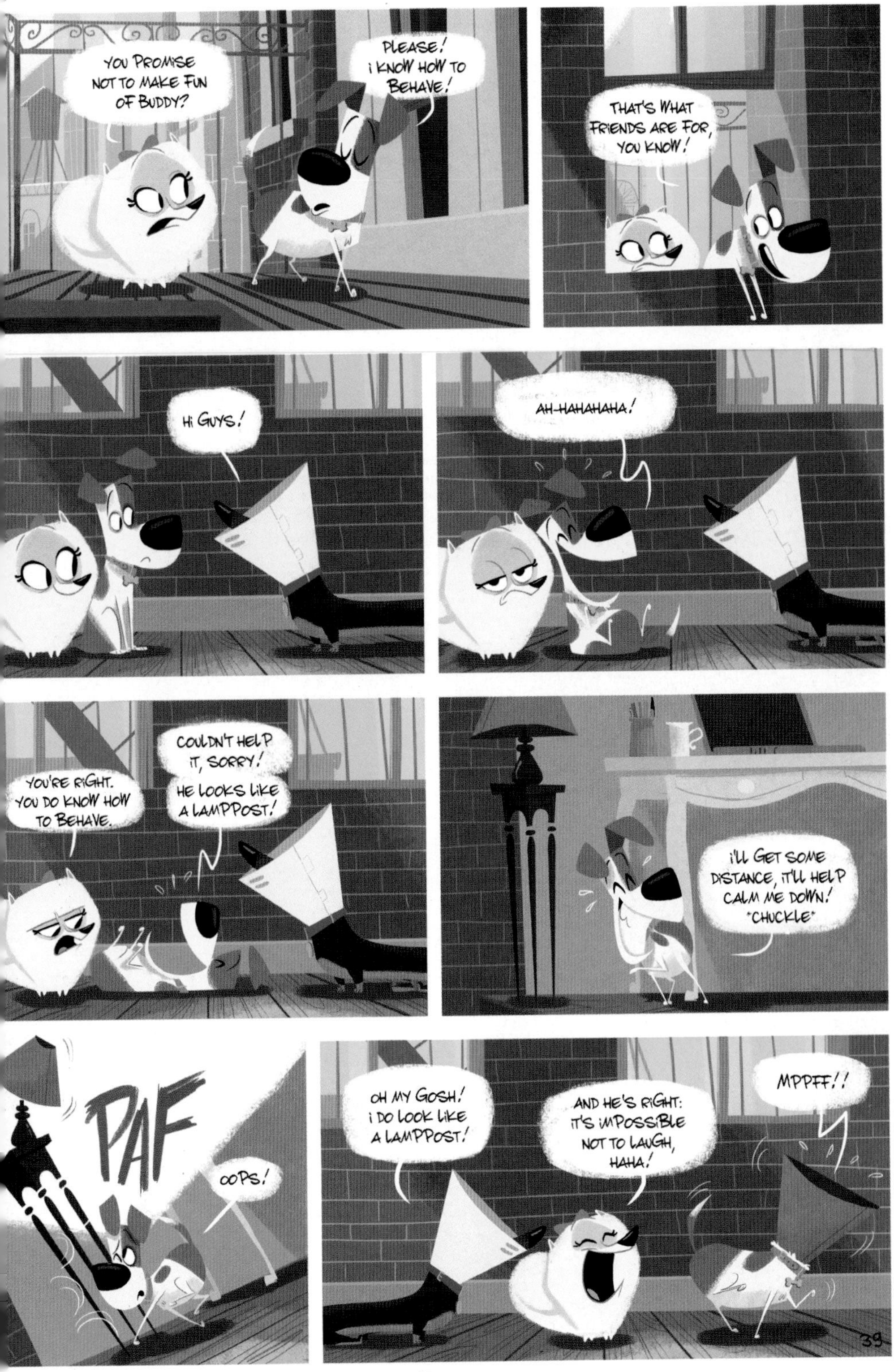
YOU PROMISE NOT TO MAKE FUN OF BUDDY?
PLEASE! I KNOW HOW TO BEHAVE!
THAT'S WHAT FRIENDS ARE FOR, YOU KNOW!
HI GUYS!
AH-HAHAHAHA!
YOU'RE RIGHT. YOU DO KNOW HOW TO BEHAVE.
COULDN'T HELP IT, SORRY!
HE LOOKS LIKE A LAMPPOST!
I'LL GET SOME DISTANCE, IT'LL HELP CALM ME DOWN! *CHUCKLE*
PAF
OOPS!
OH MY GOSH! I DO LOOK LIKE A LAMPPOST!
AND HE'S RIGHT: IT'S IMPOSSIBLE NOT TO LAUGH, HAHA!
MPPFF!!
39

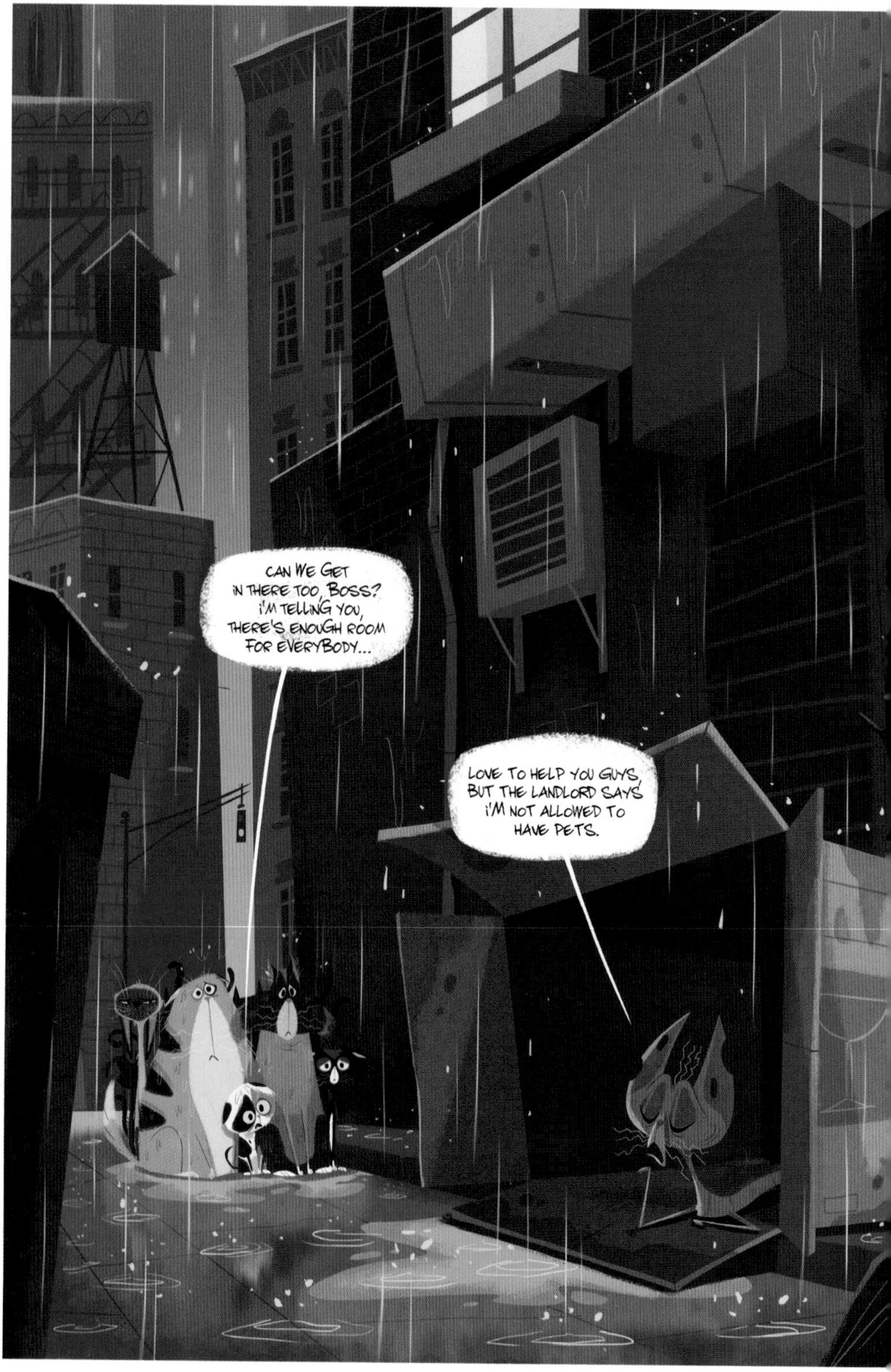
CAN WE GET IN THERE TOO, BOSS? I'M TELLING YOU, THERE'S ENOUGH ROOM FOR EVERYBODY...
LOVE TO HELP YOU GUYS, BUT THE LANDLORD SAYS I'M NOT ALLOWED TO HAVE PETS.

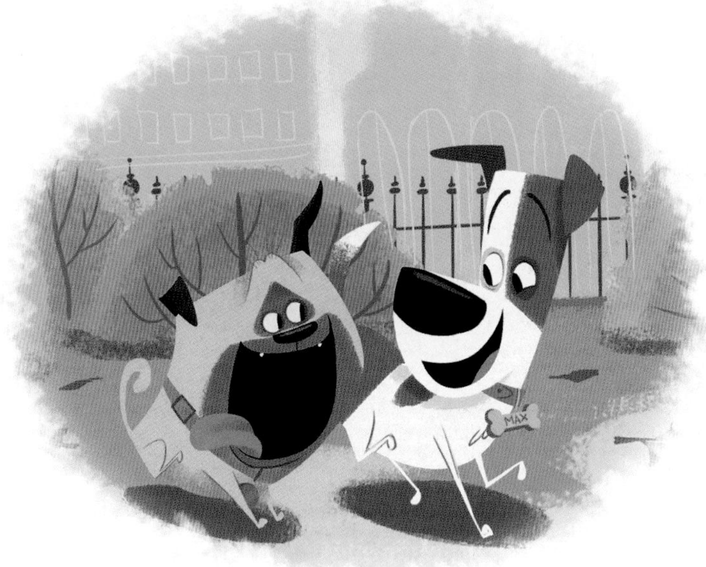
MAX

MORE MINIONS. MORE DESPICABLE!

MINIONS VOL. 1: BANANA!

Join Stuart, Kevin, Bob and the rest of the Minions for laughs and gags as the Minions unleash their unique brand of mayhem on the world.

Softcover | $6.99 | £4.99
ISBN: 9781782765547
OUT NOW

MINIONS VOL. 2: EVIL PANIC

While the villain Gru is busy taking over the world, his mischievious Minions embark on a journey of their own, fending off the evil Minions as they go about their work.

Softcover | $6.99 | £4.99
ISBN: 9781782765554
OUT NOW

MINIONS: VIVA LA BOSS

Hold on to your bananas - the Minions are back! Back for more! More chaotic catastrophes! More astonishing journeys!

Softcover | $6.99 | £5.99
ISBN: 9781787730175
OUT NOW

ALSO AVAILABLE IN HARDBACK!